A TRU

Letting out a ~~long~~ ~~c~~ ~~~~ ~~~~ paho launched himself in Calamity's direction. At the same moment, her right hand left the carbine, flying downwards—and hit the empty lip of her holster.

Suddenly, with sickening impact Calamity recalled that she had handed her Navy Colt to young John Browning and had not asked for it back before diving from the stagecoach. To make matters worse, she did not even collect her whip.

Nearer rushed the brave. One way or another, he had to be stopped. But Calamity did not fancy trying it with her bare hands.

Thrusting herself from the rock, Calamity landed facing the Arapaho. She crouched slightly and measured the distance. Before the brave could catch his balance or halt his forward rush, he blundered by her. Spinning, Calamity swung up the Winchester and smashed its metal-shot butt plate behind his shoulder.

The brave did not go down. Instead, he brought himself to a halt and turned on Calamity.

"Solly!" she cried out. "My gun's broke!"

One glance told Cole all. But all he could do was toss his rifle through the air . . .

J.T. EDSON

THE ROAD TO RATCHET CREEK

HarperTorch
An Imprint of HarperCollinsPublishers

This is a work of fiction. Names, characters, places, and incidents are products of the author's imagination or are used fictitiously and are not to be construed as real. Any resemblance to actual events, locales, organizations, or persons, living or dead, is entirely coincidental.

HARPERTORCH
An Imprint of HarperCollins*Publishers*
10 East 53rd Street
New York, New York 10022-5299

Copyright © 1968 by J.T. Edson
Originally published in the UK as *Calamity Spells Trouble*
ISBN-13: 978-0-06-078420-1
ISBN-10: 0-06-078420-2

First HarperTorch paperback printing: December 2005

Printed in the United States of America

Visit HarperTorch on the World Wide Web at www.harpercollins.com

10 9 8 7 6 5 4 3 2 1

As my life has on two occasions depended upon the reliability of his inventions, I gratefully dedicate this book to the memory of the greatest, most brilliant and prolific designer of firearms the world has ever seen, or will ever see:

JOHN MOSES BROWNING.

Author's note: I apologize to John Berns of Berns-Martin for Solly Cole's gunrig and ask him to regard it as a tribute to his own holster which is, in the words of "Davo" Davidson, "a real fine piece of work."

Chapter 1

YOUNG LADY WITH A WHIP

❧

STANDING ON THE SIDEWALK, HUGHIE RINTEL nudged his companion, Chub Farn, in the ribs and nodded toward a boy of their own age who came along the street in their direction. The chubby, sullen-faced fifteen year old boy darted a precautionary glance to make sure that his father stood with the other loafers idling their time before Promontory's Wells Fargo office. Assured of parental protection should the need arise, Hughie prepared to commence what had become his favorite sport since settling in Utah Territory.

"Yah, John Mormon!" he yelled at the boy. "How many wives's your pappy got at home?"

"Bet it's four or five at least," the tall, gangling

Chub went on loudly. "And maybe ten-fifteen each brothers 'n' sisters."

A burst of laughter far in excess of the humor of the two remarks burst from the grown-up loafers. Stocky, surly-looking Bernie Rintel—an older, even more truculent version of his son—nudged his nearest crony in the ribs and grinned approval of Hughie's actions. Much of Rintel's bullying nature had passed down to his offspring, to flourish unchecked under parental condonation and protection against the consequences of numerous misdeeds. Being a man of some influence in his section of the community, Rintel smothered any protests about his son's behavior; a fact Hughie made the most of.

Without his father's presence, Hughie would probably have thought twice before picking on that particular Mormon boy, even given Chub Farn's backing. Possessing a broad streak of discretion, Hughie preferred to take as few chances as possible in his bullying activities and the Mormon looked like he could prove a tough nut to crack.

An inch taller than Chub, the Mormon boy had a broad-shouldered and muscular frame. The round-topped black hat perching on recently-trimmed brown hair was, like his shirt collar and tie, clearly an item of clothing not usually worn. His young frame appeared to be rapidly outgrowing the home-spun brown suit. A carpetbag swung from his left hand while his right gripped what looked like an old, long-barrelled Kentucky rifle. Sufficient similar weapons could still be seen around in the early 1870's for it to attract no interest. Yet an observant onlooker might have noticed that it did not carry a ramrod under the barrel, or might have thought the aperture in the breech's sidewall unusual for what appeared to be a muzzle-loading weapon. For the rest, the gun had its hammer on the underside just ahead of the triggerguard, and looked well-used but as though it received careful maintenance and attention.

Not being observant, Hughie saw only the bare essentials. He ignored the rifle as a factor, feeling sure its owner would not dare make use of it. After rapid thought, he concluded that between them he and Chub ought to be able to handle the other boy; and Pa could be relied upon to step in should the going get too rough.

Although his tanned face reddened slightly, John Browning gave no sign of hearing the two boys' comments. The last thing he wanted was to become involved in any trouble. Even a boyish scuffle could have serious consequences if Mormon and Gentile be involved. So he continued to walk along the street, eyes fixed firmly on the sign over the Wells Fargo office building.

Encouraged by the lack of response, Hughie swung off the sidewalk so as to block John's path.

Chub followed him down, the two boys standing side by side and leering at their prospective victim.

"Where do you think you're going, Mormon?" Hughie demanded.

"To catch the south-bound stage," John answered evenly.

"What you got in the bag?" Chub asked.

"That's my business."

"Maybe it's ours too," Hughie sneered. "There's been a heap of things go missing around town."

"So we want to look what you've got in that bag," Chub went on. "My paw always says anybody that'd take four or five wives can't be trusted."

"You just open up that bag, Mormon," Hughie continued, advancing in a threatening manner. "We want to make sure you're not stealing anything."

John came to a halt, balancing lightly on his feet and watching the other two as they fanned out with the intention of taking him from either side. Still he held down his anger, although doing so took an ever increasing effort.

"I'm not looking for trouble," he warned. "All I want to do is go get a ticket and catch the stage."

"And all we want to do is look in that bag," Chub replied. "Or have you got something to hide, you stinking Mormon thief?"

"Take a look and see!" Johnny spat, swinging

up the bag and tossing it into Chub's chest. Judging by the way the skinny youngster reeled backward, the bag had a fair weight and arrived with some power.

From dealing with Chub, Johnny pivoted smoothly and launched a punch at the advancing Hughie. The sudden, effective aggression took both Gentile boys by surprise, past experience having led them to believe Mormons a meek, mild race following a policy of pacifism. So shock as much as hard knuckles colliding with some force against his chin sent Hughie staggering backward.

Swiftly Johnny stepped to the side of the street and rested his rifle against the sidewalk. Throwing aside the carpetbag, Chub leapt at John, caught him by the shoulder and turned him. For a member of a basically pacific religious creed John seemed to have considerable knowledge of defending himself. As he came around, his hand lashed out. Travelling faster than the blow Chub swung, John's fist hit its mark first and rammed its knuckles solidly against the other's nose. Although Chub's punch landed against John's cheek, pain in his nasal organ caused it to lose most of its power. It did, however, distract John long enough for Hughie to sneak in and thump him savagely across the back, propelling him into Chub's arms.

While John and Chub struggled with each

other, Hughie ran forward, sprang into the air and landed with both feet on the rifle. Not a new weapon, its cherrywood stock could no longer take such an abuse. With a crack it split across the small of the butt and then broke in two pieces held together only by the screws of the triggerguard.

John let out a howl of rage, hurled Chub away from him and flung himself at Hughie. Reaching over the hitching rail, Rintel Senior caught John's collar in passing to halt his forward progress. With a twisting heave, the man sent John staggering into the center of the street. Bounding after him, Chub turned and hit him. The blow knocked John back toward Hughie who locked both arms around him from behind. Pinning John's arms to his side, Hughie clung on grimly and yelled for Chub to fix his wagon good.

After wiping at his nose and studying the blood on the back of his hand, Chub advanced to rip a punch into Johnny's belly. As a grunt of pain rose from the trapped boy, Chub drove his fist into John's face. Knowing the reputation of Hughie's father, and the general feeling of the audience where Mormons were concerned, Chub expected no interference while beating the helpless youngster up. So feeling a hand clamp hold of his shoulder and heave him backward came as something of a surprise.

Jerked away from John, Chub felt himself swung and released with sufficient force to be sent sprawling across to the center of the street. He landed on hands and knees, twisting around to see who dared Rintel Senior's wrath and to go against public opinion in such a manner. What he saw handed him almost as great a shock as the unexpected assault.

Although clad in male clothing, Chub's assailant was a woman. Mighty unconventional, maybe, but as female as Eve. A battered U.S. cavalry kepi perched at a jaunty angle on a mop of shortish, curly red hair. Good-looking without being out-and-out beautiful, the young woman's freckled face might normally be merry and bubbling with a love of life, but right then was set in an expression of grim determination and cold contempt. She wore a fringed buckskin jacket over an open-necked dark blue shirt that, like her levis pants, looked to have been bought a size too small and shrunk in washing. Both items clung to her shapely body in a manner calculated to dispel any lingering doubts as to her sex. From the kepi to the low-heeled riding boots on her feet she was all and every inch a woman despite the way she dressed. Around her waist hung a gunbelt with an ivory-handled Colt 1861 Navy revolver riding butt forward in its contoured holster at the right side. A freighter's bull whip, its long lash coiled neatly, was thrust into a loop on the left side of her waist belt.

If Chub had been older he might have felt more

appreciation for the rich swell of the girl's breasts as they forced against the material of the shirt, its neck open low enough to allow a tantalizing glimpse of the valley between them. Five foot seven or so in height, she had a robust figure that slimmed naturally at the waist then curved out to shapely hips and legs that would not have disgraced many a female theatrical performer. Being at an age which did not yet feel the allure of female pulchritude, Chub regarded the girl as no more than a nosey interloper who ought to be taught the error of her ways.

Hughie reached the same conclusion as his friend. Shoving John aside, he flung himself at the girl. On the sidewalk Rintel's scowl at the girl's intervention changed to an indulgent grin, although his son acted in a manner to which most parents would have strenuously objected. With the Mormon boy sunk dazed on to his hands and knees, Chub and Hughie between them should be able to hand the interfering girl her needings. So Rintel stood back and did no more than comment to his friends that "this" should be worth watching.

And so it proved, although not in the way Rintel anticipated.

On a couple of occasions Hughie had seen hair-yanking brawls between saloon-girls and they did not leave him with much respect for feminine fighting ability. Unfortunately the girl he attacked did not follow the general female trend. Before

Hughie could lay hands on her, she side-stepped him with the ease of a matador avoiding the charge of an inexperienced bull. As he blundered by, she hit him in the stomach. Not a dainty tap, nor a wild, girlish swing, but a full-bodied punch as good as many a man could deliver. Hughie's breath burst from his lungs as he jackknifed over, reeled past the girl and collapsed to his knees, clutching at his mid-section.

With a bellow of rage, Rintel bounded from the sidewalk and gave the girl a shove which sent her staggering.

"No lousey lobby-lizzy's going to rough-handle my boy!" he roared and started after the girl with the view of emphasizing his point.

While still reeling from the push, she sent her right hand across to grip the whip's handle. Catching her balance, she slid free the whip and loosed its lash in a significantly competent manner. If Rintel believed that he merely faced a freight-outfit's camp-follower, dressed in male clothing for some obscure reason, he rapidly discovered his mistake. As she came to a halt, the girl measured the distance separating her from Rintel, took certain other factors quickly into consideration and acted. Life came into the bull whip's twenty foot lash and it curled toward the man like a diamondback rattlesnake hunting a jackrabbit, wrapping around his right ankle. She could hardly have timed her move better, for Rintel stood on his right leg, the left raised in a forward step. So he was in no position to resist the sudden tug she gave on the whip handle. His right foot also left the ground and he lit down flat on his back with a satisfactory thud.

With a yell that sounded three-parts fear, Chub charged toward the girl. At the same time John thrust himself to his feet and dived forward to tackle Chub around the waist and they went down in a wild, fist-flying melee.

Deftly flicking her whip free, the girl looked contemptuously at Rintel Senior and Junior. Hughie remained on his knees, clutching his belly and giving a hideous wail designed to make the onlookers regard him with sympathy. Spluttering curses, the father sat up. Rage turned his normally red face a shade of purple and he glared at his cronies.

"Get hold of her!" he yelled.

Most of the assembled men owed Rintel favors and he was a man who expected a return of any service, no matter how small, he rendered. However all but one of them drew the line at repaying favors when there might be some considerable risk of injury to their own persons involved. The exception may have felt himself more deeply in Rintel's debt than his companions, or labored under the delusion that luck alone guided the whip's lash to such a providential mark. Whatever his motives, he sprang boldly from the sidewalk and returned to it, if anything, even faster.

Pivoting smoothly around, the girl again sent her whip's lash hissing out. If the first effort had been no more than luck, the good fortune stayed with her. With the crack like a revolver shot, the lash ripped the man's hat from his head and sent it spinning away, causing his rapid withdrawal.

"Come on then, you stinking, pot-bellied, sidewalk cow-dung droppings!" the girl challenged. "Only it'll be a damned sight rougher than standing and watching a kid beat up."

Male pride and Rintel's accusing eyes caused another of the party to attempt to accept the challenge. Believing her attention to be elsewhere, he placed his hand on the hitching rail and started to vault over it. The girl's whip licked around, propelling the popper at the tip of the lash on to the rail not more than an inch from his hand. Even more than the sound of its arrival, the sight of the way it carved a groove into the stout timber made him change his mind. Already in the process of leaping over the rail, he tried to halt his progress and committed the folly of jerking his supporting hand away. With a yell he fell on to the rail and bounced from there to the sidewalk.

Again and again the whip cracked, until it became apparent to the watching men that the girl handled it with all the skill of an experienced

freight-wagon driver. Nor did any of the men regard it as a toy, although it looked somewhat
lighter, if not shorter, than the usual freighter's
implement. So effective a barrage of explosive
cracking swings did she make that at first none of
the men stood a chance of earning Rintel's gratitude by carrying out his request.

Snaking forward like a living extension of the
girl's right arm, the tip of the lash struck the sidewalk's plank and a man stamped on it. Rintel saw
his chance and took it. Although he had regained
his feet, he too had failed to break through the
deadly defense of the whip. Swiftly he lunged,
caught hold of the trapped lash and tugged at it
with the intention of wrenching it from the girl's
hand. Instead the pull had the effect of dragging
her in his direction. That, Rintel concluded, would
do just as well, allowing him to get his hands on
her. Once he did so, he aimed to teach her the lesson of her life.

As she advanced toward the stocky, powerful
man, the girl let the whip's handle slip back
through her hand until she gripped its upper end.
Rintel watched her, but attached no importance to
her movement as he prepared to release the lash
and grab her. Too late he realized that she had not
only figured out his intentions but was ready to
counter them. Accelerating her advance, she arrived before Rintel saw the danger. Up and forward whipped her right arm. Caught between the

eyes with the loaded butt of the whip's handle, Rintel reeled back, banged his heels against the edge of the sidewalk and sat down hard. Jumping away, the girl tore her whip free and prepared to use it again.

Dazed by the blow, Rintel sat for a moment shaking his head. Then he recovered enough to start spluttering curses. Never had he been so humiliated, and the fact that a woman caused his discomfiture made it so much the worse to bear. All thoughts of her sex disappeared from his mind as he started to rise and reached for the revolver thrust into his waistband.

Before the girl could take any action to defend herself against the new, and more dangerous threat to her well-being, a shot crashed from the back along the street behind her. Its bullet tossed up a spurt of dirt just in front of Rintel's feet. Taken by surprise, he jerked his hand away from the gun's butt, retreated into the edge of the sidewalk and sat down involuntarily once more. His eyes went to the shooter and he did not like what he saw.

Smoke rolled lazily up from the muzzle of a revolver in the left hand of the medium-sized man who walked along the center of the street toward the loafers. A black Texas-style Stetson hat sat back on a head of rusty red hair. While not handsome, his face had a rugged attraction despite the luxuriant moustache and a solemn expression. His stocky, powerful frame was clothed in a sober black suit, one of the less formal religious sects might wear. However a stiff, two-and-a-half inch wide belt circled his waist, carrying the revolver's holster at the left side. Although he handled the gun with a casual competence, the holster rode a mite higher than the real tophands' rig and looked different in other details.

Rintel gave no thought to the holster, being more concerned with its owner. From the sober tone of his clothing and general appearance, the newcomer could easily be a Mormon. If so, that made his actions the more heinous in Rintel's eyes.

"All right, folks," the man said, bending down to haul John off the now howling and defeated Chub with his right hand although not relaxing his watch on the loafers. "Let's stop all this fooling afore somebody gets hurt real bad."

"Who the hell asked you to bill in?" Rintel snarled. The man spoke with a Texas drawl and in general the Mormon faith made least impression on the Southern States, but that did not make Rintel feel any better disposed toward him.

"Don't let the clothes fool you, brother," warned the man. "I'm 'billing in' in my official capacity as U.S. marshal for the Utah Territory, hired by the Government to keep the peace and dispense legal justice on all sides. Cole's the name. Solly Cole to my friends, none of who I see afore me, I'm right pleased to say."

Once again Rintel's hand fled from the butt of his revolver, after moving there ready to assert his superiority over the stranger. Behind him, all the other loafers put aside their thoughts of interceding on his behalf. Standing loyal and true to a friend against a Mormon or an unimportant travelling preacher was one thing; facing and threatening a U.S. marshal on his behalf was a horse of an entirely different color. Apart from in Texas—where a captain of Rangers held pride of place—a United States marshal ranked as top man in the law enforcement of every Western State or Territory, packing a whole heap of authority in his sphere of operations.

As Solly Cole stated, he had been brought in by the Governor to keep some semblance of law and order throughout the Territory. Already the transcontinental railroad had brought in many people not of the Mormon faith. Some of them wanted to live peaceably with the Latter Day Saints who had opened up the area and could claim the rights of prior occupancy. Others did not. So Solly Cole faced the problem of acting as mediator between Mormons and Gentiles in addition to his other duties. Newly arrived to the Territory, he was not known to the loafers. One thing they could guess without being told: any man hired as U.S. marshal must be tough as they come and better than fair with a gun.

Only Rintel continued to show any hostility and

he did so in the safest manner for himself. Assuming the righteously-indignant air of a tax-payer faced by one whose salary he helped to pay, he glared at Cole and pointed to the girl who stood coiling her whip with the air of one who knows the incident to be all but closed.

"If you're a U.S. marshal, why ain't you arresting that Mormon brat and her for assaulting me 'n' my kid?" Tintel demanded. "Anybody can see what she is—."

"You want for me to show you my badge?" Cole inquired sardonically, catching the girl's arm as she cut loose with a curse and started for Rintel. "Forgive him, sister, for he knoweth not what damned fool things he does, or who *you* are."

"Who is she?" asked one of the loafers.

"Miss Martha Jane Canary, brother," intoned Cole with all the solemnity of a newly-appointed bishop addressing a rich congregation. "Or, to a bunch of ignorant bastards like you, Calamity Jane."

Chapter 2

TO ERR IS HUMAN

———◦◦◦———

HEARING THE GIRL'S NAME EXPLAINED A WHOLE HEAP of things to the watching, listening and impressed loafers. All now saw why she came to be dressed in that unconventional manner and showed such dexterity in the use of the long-lashed bull whip.

Although some of the stories going the rounds about her were pure fabrication, Miss Martha Jane Canary could claim to be something of a legend in her own young life-time. She was not a rich Eastern girl come to the Western plains to forget a broken romance, or the daughter of a famous plainsman and his Indian princess wife (despite both stories having appeared about her in issues of the *Police Gazette*). The truth, while less romantic, would have made just as dramatic and entertaining a tale.

On the way West in search of a new home, Martha Jane's father died. Finding herself unable to support a family of three young children, Charlotte Canary left them in a St. Louis convent and continued on her way. There was too much of her mother's restless spirit in Martha Jane for her to accept the discipline of the convent. On her sixteenth birthday, she slipped off and stowed away in one of Dobe Killem's freight wagons.

Discovered at the end of the first day's journey, the girl might have been returned to St. Louis immediately but for the indisposition of Killem's cook. One of the few things the nuns had managed to instill in Martha Jane had been a thorough knowledge of cooking. Setting to, she prepared a good meal for the hungry men of the outfit and earned herself a ride to the next town. Due to various incidents along the way, Martha Jane not only endeared herself to Killem's roughneck drivers but also came to be regarded as something of a lucky charm. By the time they reached the town, Martha Jane found herself adopted as one of the outfit.

During that, and subsequent trips, the men taught Martha Jane their trade. She learned to care for and drive a six-horse team, to maintain a wagon, handle firearms with some skill and to wield a bull whip equally well as a means of equine inducement or as a weapon.

Travelling the Great Plains with the freight outfit, her education naturally took in other basic, but vitally important matters. She knew how to live off the land and possessed some skill in the healing arts, using remedies picked up from Indian medicine women and other such practitioners. Entering saloons with the other drivers brought her into conflict with the female employees, so she quickly became adept at defending herself in cat-clawing brawls. Leading a healthier life than the average saloongirl, in addition to having received instruction in both fist and roughhouse fighting from the men of the outfit, she started with an edge over her opponents. So far she had not been defeated in a fight.*

A good-hearted, happy-go-lucky girl, Martha Jane had developed a penchant for becoming involved in any disturbance going on. Not that she looked for trouble. She never needed to, it found her like a spawning salmon locating the river of its birth. So much so that her given name rapidly was forgotten and she gained the name Calamity Jane.

Returning her whip to its sling on the waist belt, Calamity walked over to where John stood holding the rifle and staring at its fractured butt. Apart

---

*The story of Calamity's defeat is told in THE WILDCATS.

from a bleeding nose, the boy looked no worse for his beating. However his suit bore a coating of street-dust and he appeared to have lost his back-stud, for the collar stood clear of the shirt.

"How bad did they hurt you?" she asked.

"N—Not bad, ma'am," he replied. "Look at this!"

"Yeah!" Calamity said angrily. "That lard-gutted yahoo did it deliberate. Say, is there anything bust-able in your bag?"

Clearly John had been more concerned with the condition of his rifle than over the remainder of his belongings. Putting aside the rifle, he collected the bag. Blood from his nose dribbled into the bag as he drew open its top and studied the contents, so he shut it again hurriedly.

"It's all right, ma'am."

"Come on then. I've got something to fix your nose like new."

John dabbed an oil-stained handkerchief on his nose, studied the blood it gathered and glared at the blubbering Hughie who still knelt in the street.

"Maybe I ought to——."

"And maybe you oughtn't," grinned Calamity. "You come with me, if that's all right with the marshal."

"I'd say 'yes' to that, sister," Cole replied. "Unless this gent here wants to take action against you under the legal law."

"What if I do?" growled Rintel hopefully.

"Then I'll do my duty, brother," Cole assured him. "Only I'll take you to the pokey with them."

"What for?"

"Assaulting the lady, to wit, shoving hell out of her on the street as a starter. Making a public nuisance. Wouldn't even be surprised if she couldn't have that miserable sinner who stomped on her whip throwed in for damage to her rightful owned property. You still wanting me to do something?"

"Naw!" admitted Rintel, a sullen note replacing the hope. "I don't."

"Now there's truly true Christian generosity, brother," drawled Cole. "Like the Good Book says, to err is human, to forgive when things could go wrong if you don't shows right good sense."

While accepting Cole's version of Alexander Pope's wise saying as something from the Bible, Calamity felt it hardly covered all the affair.

"Forgiving's fine, marshal," she said. "But that Jasper's son bust the boy here's rifle."

"There's that," Cole agreed.

"Hell, it's only a busted up old relic——," began Rintel.

"And it's still the boy's property," Cole reminded him.

Some Mormons resented the coming of the Gentiles to their land and, given the chance, showed much the same kind of bigotry that other people practiced toward them; but not John's father. A shrewd man, he knew there could be no stopping the arrival of non-Saints and had always advocated living peaceably with the newcomers. In addition he had taught his sons to avoid leaving hard feelings when in contact with even hostile Gentiles. So John made a decision. Removing the handkerchief from his face, he looked at the marshal.

"It's all right, sir," he said. "I can fix this up, it's only the wood that's bust."

"If that's the way you want it, boy," Cole replied.

"That's the way I want it," Johnny insisted.

"Then we can all part friends," the marshal said.

"I'm all for friendship," Calamity remarked, laying a hand on John's shoulder. "Come on, friend."

With that she steered him to his property and when he had gathered both rifle and bag, headed him down the street. A bedroll stood on the sidewalk with a Winchester Model 1866 carbine resting against it. From the way Calamity went to and picked them up, John concluded that she owned them, having left them there when she came to his aid. Regaining possession of her property, she walked with the boy toward the Wells Fargo office. Instead of entering the building, she took him to the rear and told him to wash off in the horsetrough.

Removing his collar with an air of relief, John obeyed the order. Although he cleaned off the dirt collected during the fight, his nose still bled. Calamity appeared to expect this, for she stood alongside her open bedroll and held what looked like a horn snuffbox.

"Set on the side and tilt your head back," she ordered. "And, afore you ask, this stuff I'm going to use's powdered witch-hazel leaves."

"Ma always uses it to stop bleeding," John replied as he followed her instructions.

"Which only proves that all women have better sense than men, most times," Calamity told him, deftly shooting some of the powder up each of his nostrils. "Now sniff her up as high as she'll go."

John did as ordered, feeling his nose clog up as the powder and blood mingled. After fighting down a desire to sneeze, he wrinkled his face and reached up a hand to touch the nose. Letting out a snort, Calamity flicked his hand away.

"Damn it all, boy," she objected. "I put that stuff there to do something. Leave it have time to work."

"Sure, Miss Calamity."

"And don't call me 'miss,' or 'ma'am,' you make me feel old. The name's Calam—to my friends."

"Yes'm, M—Calam," Johnny said, trying to avoid twitching his nose and ejecting the powder.

"My name's Browning, John Moses Browning,
M—Calam."

"You'd be kin to Jonathan Browning, the Ogden
gunsmith, I'd say," the girl acknowledged, shaking hands as formally as two bankers meeting to
discuss a loan.

"He's my pappy."

"I've never met him, but my boss allows he's the
best gunsmith west of the Big Muddy. Say, that's
one of his old slide-rifles ain't it?"

"Yes," John agreed, pride showing on his face.

Stepping forward, the girl picked up the old rifle and looked at it. Considering the primitive conditions under which it had been made, it showed
very good workmanship. That fact interested
Calamity less than the principle on which the rifle
worked. It had been one of the first successful
repeating-fire shoulder-arms—as opposed to
revolvers—to be made and it was Jonathan
Browning's own invention, possessing a capacity
for continuous discharge unequalled in the days
before metal-case ammunition. Its magazine was
a rectangular iron bar with holes—from five to
twenty-five depending on the customers' needs—
drilled in to take the loose powder, ball and percussion cap. After sliding the bar into the breech
aperture, the user pressed a small lever on the
right side of the frame, moving the magazine forward, lining the first chamber with the barrel and
ensuring a gas-tight seal. Each pressure of the

lever moved the bar along to the next chamber, while the under-hammer permitted easy cocking without removing the butt from the shoulder.

Despite its simplicity of mechanism, lack of production facilities prevented Browning from making a significant number of rifles. At the time he was also mainly concerned with supplying arms for the Mormons' departure from an unfriendly East, so few reached Gentile hands. Before he could settle down and build a factory capable of turning out his rifles in quantity, B. Tyler Henry's improvements on metal-case cartridges rendered percussion-fired rifles, even a successful repeater, obsolete. Browning found too much with which to occupy himself in Utah and could no longer spare the time to dabble in inventing or making guns.

"That damned fool kid!" Calamity said, examining the broken butt. "He's ruined a good gun."

"It can easy be fixed," John assured her. "When I get back, I'll have Brother Matt whomp up a new butt and fit it on."

"Are you learning to be a gunsmith like your pappy, Johnny?"

"Yes'm," he replied with enthusiasm.

Learning might be something of an understatement, for he had been involved in his father's work since he could first hold a tool and follow an order. Shortly after his thirteenth birthday he had made his first gun, using old parts retrieved from the shop's junk-pile. While that gun did not prove a great success, his next effort, recently completed, could stand up alongside the rifles produced by some of the smaller firearms factories which had sprung up back East.

"It's a good trade," Calamity stated. "And one that'll allus be needed. Maybe one day you'll be as good at it as your pappy."

"I sure hope so," John answered. "What're you doing in Promontory, Calam?"

"I'm catching the noon stage out too."

"Driving it?"

"Naw!" she snorted, grinning to show him that her disgust was at the thought of a freight wagon driver handling the ribbons on anything as cissified as a stagecoach. "I'm headed for Ratchet Creek on a chore for my boss. Come here by train and couldn't find a hoss worth a cuss in the livery barns, so I'm riding the stage. I sure hope none of the outfit hear about it."

"I'm going to Ratchet Creek myself," Johnny told her.

"That's a tolerable long trip for a b——," Calamity began, then stopped as she saw him stiffen slightly, and made a correction, "young feller. Are you visiting kin?"

"Nope. Pappy's sending me to buy up some machinery we saw when we went down there in the spring. We'd gone down for a couple of week's hunting and wound up doing gun repairs most all the time."

"That's allus the way," smiled the girl. "Let's take a look at what we'll be riding in, shall we, afore we go buy our tickets."

Carrying their belongings, Calamity and Johnny walked over to where the stagecoach stood alongside the corral which held its team of six light draft horses. In the days before the completion of the transcontinental railroad the stage they approached had made the "Big Run" which followed the old Pony Express route from St. Joseph to San Francisco via Julesberg, Forts Laramie and Bridger and Salt Lake City. With its team of specially bred horses, it still offered the fastest, most comfortable means of transport, other than the railroad, out West and reached towns that its new competitor did not touch.

The thorough-braced coach they looked at had been manufactured by the New England company of Abbot & Downing, designed for its specific work over the miles of rolling, almost roadless plains country. To hold down the weight, the minimum of metal went into the construction, only the finest Norwegian iron being used. Mostly the body work consisted of carefully laminated and dried sheets of plywood, but the oak or linden timber used as supports had been cut and allowed to age for not less than four years before the makers regarded it as suitable. The thorough-braces which supported the roughly egg-shaped body above the draft and running gear were of the finest, stoutest leather produced by the master tanners Lynn and Framingham, no less than eight specially selected steer hides going into the making of a single coach. The yellow-spoked wheels of handhewn ash could not be bettered. Nor had leaving the "Big Run" caused any neglect of the outward appearance. All signs of past mishaps, bullet or arrow holes and the like, had been removed or covered, and the original vermillion paint of the body-work was kept fresh as was the yellow and black trim of the running gear. Even the New England landscape scenes by artists John and Edwin Burgum were replaced as needed.

Weighing slightly over two thousand pounds, the coach could carry up to fifteen passengers and around a ton of baggage. It would cover at least twenty-five miles in a full day's travel, given reasonably decent trails. Leaving Promontory at noon, it would reach Ratchet Creek in two and a half days, each night being spent at a company way station.

Seeing Calamity and John examining his coach and team, the driver ambled toward them. Naturally such a magnificent vehicle as a Wells Fargo Concord stage from the "Big Run" could not be driven by any ordinary mortal, so all the drivers tended to show a certain eccentricity in their choice of clothing. Unlike many of his colleagues, who tended to be stylish if not outright dandified in their dress, the short, wiry old timer wore fringed buckskins in the fashion of the departed Mountain Men. White hair hung shoulder long from beneath his coonskin cap and a long moustache curled its ends like the horns of a buffalo. Indian moccasins covered his feet. His wampum-coated gunbelt carried a bowie knife at the left and a Walker Colt swung its long, heavy weight at the right. Trailing from the belt were five hanks of hair believed to be scalps taken from Indians or outlaws foolish enough to interfere with his coach.

"Come to see a real rig, Calam gal?" he asked.

Slowly the girl turned and studied the speaker. Despite his belligerent and war-like bearing, she snorted her deep disgust.

"Near on twenty cents a mile and they give us a creaking packing-box lousy with dry-rot to ride in," she told John in a loud voice, " 'navvies' to haul it and a worn-out ole goat who's blind as a snubbing post to drive it."

John gulped and prepared to duck for cover. Handling the ribbons of a "Big Run" stagecoach was not work for a meek, mild-natured man and those who did it developed a pride of occupation second to none. No driver worth his salt would tamely accept adverse criticism of his vehicle or person; while to refer to his highly-prized team as "navvies"—short for Navajo Indian ponies, by repute the poorest specimens of horse-flesh on earth—was as risky as accusing the average Texan of voting Republican. However the old-timer merely eyed Calamity up and down in a superior manner, only to be equalled by the captain of a U.S. Navy first-rate battleship studying the skipper of a small, unimportant coastal boat.

"Don't pay her any mind, boy," he told John. "It's only envy 'cause she's never handled nothing but a bunch of lead-footed hauling hosses and a stove-up ole wagon. Why'n't you come along and see what it feels like to ride behind a bunch of real hosses, Calam?"

"I would," she replied. "Only I've got to come with you instead. Which same I'd thought twice about it had I known you was to be on the box. Johnny, this here's Pizen Joe. Joe, get acquainted with young Johnny Browning from Ogden way."

"Know ye pappy, boy," the old timer greeted, extending a gnarled old hand which still possessed a powerful grip. His sharp eyes raked over John's face and he went on, "You been in a fight?"

"Yes, sir," John answered apologetically.

"Can't say as it surprises me, company you're keeping," Joe sniffed. "That fool Calamity'd pick a fussing with her echo if there warn't nobody else around. Still, I allus says you can't judge a feller by the company he keeps."

"You'd be a lonely man if folks did," Calamity put in.

"Reckon I'll ask 'em for another shotgun mes-

senger along happen you're riding with us,
Calam," Joe said.

"Yah!" Calamity scoffed. "You're safe. I'd want
somebody a whole heap younger 'n' better looking than you was I hunting a husband."

"Which same I'm surely pleasured that I ain't
younger 'n' better-looking then," Joe cackled.
"Anyways, I can't spend all day standing here
whittle-whanging with you. There's some of us
has work to do."

"You must know him real good to talk like that
about his coach and hosses," Johnny remarked as
he watched the old timer walk off toward the office building.

"We've run across each other here and there,"
admitted Calamity, also following Pizen Joe's departure and smiling. "He's as good as the best of
'em, Johnny boy and don't let his looks fool you.
Maybe he's getting along in years, but his horns
ain't been sawed off by a good country mile."

Which meant, as John knew, that Pizen Joe still
retained the means to defend his fiery nature and
peppery tongue despite the advancing years.
Then the boy's eyes went to Calamity and he
smiled. Between her and the old driver, unless
John missed his guess, the ride to Ratchet Creek
ought to be a trip to be remembered.

Chapter 3

WHEN STRUCK, TURN THE OTHER CHEEK

❦

DESPITE HER FRIENDSHIP WITH PIZEN JOE AND PRO-
fessed faith in his ability as a driver, Calamity sat a
mite tense in her seat when the stagecoach rolled
out beyond Promontory's city limits. She never felt
completely at ease when riding in a vehicle that
somebody else drove.

Although the coach rocked and swayed over
the uneven hooves- and wheel-rutted surface of
the trail, the effective springing of its thorough-
bracing saved the passengers from the spine-
jarring bumps of less well-designed vehicles.
There were only five other passengers making the
first leg of the trip, allowing plenty of room to sit
in comfort. Their baggage rode on top, or in the
boot at the rear. However the Wells Fargo Com-

pany did not expect its paying guests to be separated from their weapons, so the company fitted racks above the seats to accommodate such rifles, shotguns or carbines as the passengers might have along, saving them from the necessity of sitting and holding the shoulder arms throughout the trip.

To help ease her tension, Calamity turned her attention to the other occupants of the coach. At her right side sat John Browning, on her left a small, petite young woman. Facing them were Marshal Solly Cole and a pair of travelling salesmen, tall, heavily built men wearing check suits, darby hats, cravats with imitation diamond stickpins, their reddened faces bearing expressions of professional joviality calculated to put prospective customers at ease and in a buying mood. So far there had been little or no conversation. Cole gave no sign of knowing Calamity or John and the drummers spent their time eyeing the girls with frank interest.

Calamity did not object to being studied and admitted that the other girl rated male interest. Unless Calamity missed her guess, being stared at by men was no novelty to the other female traveller. A dainty, impractical hat perched on piled-up black hair. With just sufficient make-up to emphasize its best points, the girl's beautiful face had a continental appearance. Small she might be, but the figure under the elegant, if slightly risque travelling suit appeared to be rich and full. Calamity was willing to bet that the girl had theatrical connections and expected to hear either a real or assumed French accent when she spoke.

From the girl, Calamity turned to Marshal Cole as he sat under his Winchester Model 1866 rifle. After wondering if he was really as sober and religious as he sounded, and also where he recognized her from, she dropped her eyes to his gunbelt and studied the holster in particular. Instead of being cut down to leave clear access to the revolver's triggerguard, its side rose high enough to obscure it. Another point struck her as she looked—the holster appeared to have split open down its front. Closer examination told her this had been done deliberately, the gun being held horizontally by a finely-tempered steel spring-clip gripping its cylinder inside the leather and its vertical position retained by the muzzle of the barrel resting in a shaped slot in the holster's bottom plug. Used to the conventional type of gun rig, she wondered what advantages, if any, Cole's holster offered, but did not raise the point.

At Calamity's side John studied Cole's gunbelt, although his interest centered on the weapon it held. His eyes took in the bell-shaped, square-bottomed, oil-finished black walnut grips, different in shape to the hand-fitting curve of a Colt's butt. Nor did any holster-size Colt at that time have a solid frame and the gun in Cole's holster had a metal bar over the cylinder. At first John thought it to be a Remington, then decided it was not. While wanting to satisfy his curiosity, he wondered how he might obtain the required information without offending its owner. Sucking in a breath, he took the plunge.

"I've never seen a revolver like that before, sir," he said.

"It's a Rogers & Spencer Army Model, son," Cole replied indulgently. "I needed a gun in a hurry one time and this was the only one on hand. Got to like its hang and balance, so I never bothered to make a change."

"Don't often see a deacon wearing a gun," the brown haired drummer put in. "I thought you fellers were men of peace."

"The Good Book says when struck, turn the other cheek, brother," Cole answered. "Only if somebody hits that one as well, I reckon a man's got to do something about it."

"Hallelujah!" grinned the other salesman. "The world'd sure be a heap safer place if nobody had guns."

"Now that's the living truth," agreed Cole and directed a wink in John's direction. "Only as long as thieves can lay hands on 'em I reckon there'd be nothing more foolish than stopping honest folks owning one."

On hearing Cole addressed as "deacon," John felt indignant at the thinly-veiled mockery of the

speaker and opened his mouth to correct the
drummer. He caught Calamity's elbow in the ribs
hard enough to halt the words unsaid. A glance at
the girl told him that her move had been no accident. Looking at Cole, he realized that the marshal
not only saw but approved of Calamity's action.

Once started, the conversation continued and
the passengers introduced themselves. As
Calamity expected, the other girl spoke with a
slight, but attractive, French accent. She told them
her name was Monique de Monsarrat, that she
worked as a singer, lived in Ratchet City and had
been appearing in the Bon Ton Theater at
Promontory. The brown-haired drummer claimed
to be Wally Conway and represented a St. Louis
cutlery manufacturer. His companion was Lou
Thorbold, selling gentlemen's toilet goods. While
Calamity and Johnny gave their correct names,
Cole let the others believe him to be a travelling
deacon called Rand.

Toward three in the afternoon Pizen Joe brought
his team to a halt by a small stream. Telling the
passengers to light and rest their butt-ends, with a
muttered apology to Monique for mentioning
such a subject in a lady's presence, the old timer
and his guard set about watering the horses.

"He never apologized to me," grinned
Calamity.

"Maybe he's done like the Good Book says,"

Cole replied. "Thou art weighed in the balances and sure been found fit to ride the river with."

"Could be," she answered. "Or he don't think I'm a lady."

"There's that," admitted Cole and walked off into the bushes.

After the marshal disappeared from sight, Calamity drew John away from the other passengers and lowered her voice so that only the boy could hear her.

"You near on did a fool trick back there a piece," she told him. "Don't you ever again go butting in and telling folks when they've made mistakes. Especially when they make 'em about a gent in the marshal's line of work."

"I just thought he'd want them to know who he is," John replied.

"If he had, he stood right capable of telling 'em his-self."

"Gee! Do you reckon he's after them two drummers?"

"How'd you mean?" asked Calamity.

"Because they're wanted by the law," John clarified.

"I don't know what, or who he's after and ain't meaning to start guessing," Calamity told him. "And don't go getting all kinds of ideas that might come out wrong. One thing's plain as a crow on a snow drift though."

"What's that?"

"The marshal don't want folks to know who and what he is. Now there's nobody talks worse'n a drummer, that's how he makes his living. So most likely all the marshal don't want them to know him for is so's they can't spread word around that he's in this neck of the woods."

Put in such a manner Johnny could see that he might be doing the two salesmen a serious wrong. He also felt grateful to Calamity for steering him right in the matter. On the previous occasions when John had travelled, his father had always been along to give advice. With any other girl not more than three years his senior he would have felt irritated at receiving unrequested counsel, but not when it came from Calamity Jane.

"I'll remember it, Calam," he promised. "Say, do you reckon the marshal'll let me look closer at his gun?"

"Maybe. Only not while he's travelling. Ask him tonight at Coon Hollow way station and he might."

"We'll be moving off real soon, folks," called the guard, a tall, lean young man in range clothes and backing his low-hanging Army Colt with a twenty-inch barrelled ten gauge shotgun.

"If you want to go; Johnny boy," Calamity told the youngster, "now's the time to do it and among them there bushes's the place. I'll go further along."

While hitching up her pants after the process of "going," Calamity heard a rustle among the bushes. Even as she held up the garments with her left hand and reached for the Navy Colt, hung conveniently from a branch, Cole's voice came to her ears.

"We're all cast in the same mold, sister."

"Only the bits stick out in different places on some of us," she replied, putting both hands back to the work of adjusting her clothing.

"I wouldn't know," Cole said. "Not having looked."

Calamity believed him and his pose as a deacon had nothing to do with the decision. Having completed fastening her pants, she swung the gunbelt around her waist and buckled it into place. Then she walked from the bushes to Cole's side.

"I figured it might be one of that pair of drummers when I heard you and just recalled that I've left my whip in the stage."

"You wouldn't be forgetful enough to have forgotten to load that Colt as well, would you?" he replied.

"Happen you'd been one of them, or somebody else with wrong ideas about why I went into the bushes, you'd've right soon learned the answer to *that*."

"Is that carbine of your'n in the coach full-loaded, sister?"

"Unless some danged fool's been and emptied

all the bullets out it is," she assured him. "What's up, marshal?"

"Saw a fair slew of hoss tracks down that ways. Just hoof marks, nary a sign of a shoe among the whole boiling of 'em."

"Owlhoots?" asked Calamity hopefully and her hope did not rise from a desire to help fight off an attempt at robbing the stage.

"Not unless they went in for wearing moccasins," Cole replied. "And walked toeing in a mite."

Although Calamity showed no sign, she knew just what the marshal's words meant. While white men occasionally wore moccasins, they never walked with the toes pointing slightly inward as did every Indian. Unshod horses also pointed to the makers of the tracks belonging to one of the Indian tribes.

"Let's go lump them folks into the stage and get the hell out of here, if you'll excuse the word, pastor," said Calamity.

"It'd be best, sister," agreed Cole.

"Say," Calamity remarked as they started to walk in the direction of the stagecoach. "How'd you recognize me back in town? I'd remember you had we met."

"A kinsman of mine told me some about you. Said to watch out for a red-topped, freckle-faced hump of perversity wearing men's clothes and toting a bull whip," Cole explained. "He allowed you to be more trouble than ten drunken Texas cowhands celebrating the Battle of San Jacinto in a Kansas trail-end town."

"Who'd he be?" grinned Calamity, having seen Texans celebrate the battle which ended Mexican rule of their home State, then a province of Mexico. "It sounds like he knows me real well."

"Now I wouldn't want to be the one to judge *that*," Cole said dryly. "His name's Mark Counter."

"Ole Mark's kin of your'n?"

"Our side of the family's been trying to hide it for years, sister," Cole replied in his most solemn way, like the local preacher apologizing for his brother being the town drunk. "You know him?"

For all the solemnity Calamity caught a twinkle in the marshal's eye and felt even more certain that his entire appearance was no more than a pose. Unless her considerable knowledge of men went sadly wrong, she figured Solly Cole could be just as lively as his illustrious cousin under the right conditions.

"Let's say we've met," she answered tactfully. "Yes sir, marshal, let's just say that."*

Before they could go any further into details of Calamity's first hectic meeting with Texas cowhand, gun fighter and dandy, Mark Counter,† the

---

*Calamity's first meeting with Mark Counter is told in TROUBLED RANGE.

†Mark Counter's story can be read in the author's floating outfit stories.

stagecoach came into view. To one side of it
Monique de Monsarrat stood talking with the
drummers and Johnny appeared from among the
bushes. Pizen Joe was checking his team's harness, a precautionary measure Calamity approved
of and the guard studied the fastening of the
loaded boot.

Catching the old timer's eye as he approached,
Cole mouthed one word in barely more than a soft
whisper.

"Injuns!"

For all the difference it made to his outward appearance, Joe might not have heard the word, or
understood its meaning. Yet he turned from the
horses and called, "All in, folks. We're rolling."

Having ridden shotgun alongside the old timer
for over a year, Cultus, the guard, knew his ways.
Without waiting for a further explanation, Cultus
went toward the passengers. He started to move
them in the direction of the stage's door with all
the polite efficiency of a bouncer in a high-class
saloon easing its influential customers out at closing time. Drawing back after the drummers followed Monique and John into the coach, he
glanced inquiringly at Cole and received the same
one-word, but sufficient, explanation.

"We've had no trouble with 'em down this ways
for a spell," Cultus remarked quietly. "Which
same, afore you tell me, don't mean a thing."

"That's the living, gospel truth, brother," Cole replied. "What's ahead?"

"Much the same as we're passing through right now, most of the way. Rolling, fairly open country and a good trail that we can make some speed over."

"How about the bits that aren't 'much the same'?"

"There's a ford maybe three mile on."

"Hard to cross?" asked Calamity, an interested listener to the conversation.

"Bottom's firm, level gravel and the water'll not be more'n a couple of foot deep at this time of the year," Cultus answered.

"Then what's wrong with it?" Cole wanted to know.

"We have to roll down a slope to reach it and haul up another when we're across the other side."

"There's no other way over?"

"Not within maybe two miles up or down, marshal. Stream runs through a valley and its slopes go from real steep to straight down. So the Company allowed it'd be cheaper to cut a trail down to the ford instead of building a bridge over."

Calamity and Cole exchanged glances before the marshal asked the next question. "It'd be a good place for an ambush?"

"Too damned good," Cultus agreed. "Trail's not

wide on either side and there're some pretty hefty rocks on both sides of the stream."

"Then it'll be best if Joe stops afore we hit the top and lets us scout it on foot afore we roll through," Cole stated.

"I'm with you on that," Cultus agreed and raised his voice. "Jump on in, Calam, deacon, you're keeping us waiting."

Letting Calamity climb in first, Cole paused and turned to give the surrounding area a careful scrutiny. On following her inside, he found that she had placed John between her and Monique so as to have a seat alongside a window. Calamity directed a questioning stare at the marshal's rifle as he sat down and caught his almost imperceptible head-shake. So she let her carbine remain in its place above her, the coiled whip hanging from its barrel.

As soon as Cole closed the coach's door, Pizen Joe started the horses moving. Everything had been done so smoothly not one of the other passengers realized the true position. Monique appeared to have spent her time becoming better acquainted with the drummers and they kept up a cheerful conversation which prevented them from noticing anything changed in Calamity or Cole's behavior. If John found the girl less receptive to his questions, he attributed it to her becoming tired. One could hardly expect a woman, even Calamity

Jane, to stand up to the rigors of a long trip as well as a man, he concluded, and lapsed into silence.

Almost two miles fell behind the coach, with Calamity and Cole searching the surrounding range for the first sign of danger. Then the girl stiffened slightly in her seat and Cole, alert for any hint she might give, followed the direction of her gaze.

Topping a rim maybe a quarter of a mile from the trail, an Indian brave brought his horse to a halt. He turned, swaying visibly on his mount's back and waved excitedly. Much to Calamity's surprise, he accompanied the wave with a shout. Other braves rode into sight, milling around the first, pointing at the coach and making enough noise to reach the passengers' ears.

"Sacre bleu!" Monique gasped. "Indians!"

"They look tolerable excited," Conway went on.

At that moment one of the Indians hoisted up a familiar-looking stone jug on the crook of his arm and drank deeply of its contents. At least one other of the braves had such a jug slung across his shoulders. The sight of the jugs cleared up a few aspects of the affair which had been puzzling Calamity.

"Excited!" she spat out. "They're stunk-up drunk."

In view of the first brave's casual appearance, lack of caution and general attitude, Calamity had started to hope that his party might be no more than a group of lodge-brothers on their way to some function, or just bucks on a hunting trip. A raiding party only rarely showed themselves so openly or made sufficient noise to alert their victims. Certainly they would not have done so under the prevailing conditions. Reared from birth to be fighting men, the unlettered savages possessed as clear a knowledge of military tactics as any gained by a white officer attending West Point Military Academy. They could assess a situation and would be unlikely to throw away the element of surprise in such a manner. Nor would a party on the warpath be careless enough to leave plain tracks for possible enemies or victims to find.

Of course all that only applied to sober Indians.

Once a buck carried a belly-full of the white-eye brother's rotgut whiskey, none of the normal behavior patterns remained. The only thing one could be certain of when dealing with drunken Indians was that they could be relied upon to be fully primed and ready for any devilment.

Clearly Cole's thoughts followed much the same line as Calamity's deliberations on Indian behavior. Reaching up, he lifted his rifle free from the rack and worked its lever to throw a bullet into the chamber. Calamity took down her carbine and let the whip drop on to the seat. Good weapon that it might be under the right conditions, she could not make use of it in the confines of the coach. Then a thought hit her and she grinned at the marshal.

"What was that about letting the other feller hit you first and turning the other cheek?" she asked, feeding a bullet into the carbine's chamber.

"A good thought, sister," Cole replied. "Only it don't apply to red varmints who've been sinning by drinking strong likker. Then you should stop 'em afore they hit the first che—."

Any more he might have wished to say on the subject was chopped off abruptly as one of the bucks threw up a rifle and fired at the coach.

Chapter 4

YIELD NOT TO ANGER

❧

As the Indian's bullet struck the top of the stagecoach and whined away in a screaming ricochet, Pizen Joe took the appropriate action. Letting out a howl like a scalded cougar, the old timer made his whip crack over the heads of the two lead horses. Bred for their work, the spirited team responded with such a will that the force of their forward surge jerked the coach's wheels off the ground. From a steady trot, the pace increased to a fast gallop.

Letting out wild yells, the Indians sent their horses charging down the slope. Watching them, Calamity found any remaining doubts she might have felt about their sobriety wiped away. Every brave rode with an extra abandon and recklessness that went far beyond a mere desire to count coup on the hated white occupants of the stage coach. Even the faint hope that the bucks had no other intention than a little harmless fun, like cowhands charging into town on pay day, died with the certainty that all had been drinking. While hard liquor affected white men in various ways, from joviality to aggressiveness or maudlin sorrow, it only served to turn an Indian savage and fighting wild.

Only in one respect did the braves' inebriated condition help Calamity's party. Instead of following the wise course of descending the slope and taking up the chase along the trail, they tried to come down on it at an angle. Converging with the stage down the slope slowed the Indians' horses and made controlling them difficult, which in turn prevented the use of weapons with any hope of accuracy. Had the braves been sober, they would never have taken such a course.

"What are the, Sioux?" Thorbold demanded, producing a Smith & Wesson No. 2 revolver from under his jacket.

"Arapaho," Calamity corrected and eyed the .32 caliber handgun with faint contempt before turning to Conway. "Are you heeled, mister?"

"Sure," he replied, taking a three-inch barrelled Colt Pocket Pistol out.

"That'll spook 'em for sure," Calamity sniffed. "How about you, sister?"

"I have a Deringer in my reticule," Monique replied.

"Keep a hold on it then and use it if you have to," Calamity ordered.

"Darn it, I knew I shouldn't've left my rifle back at Promontory!" John groaned.

"It wouldn't've been much use with that busted butt," Calamity pointed out and drew her Colt. "Do you know how to use this?"

"Yes'm."

"Then get to the other window and be ready to do it."

"They're on this side," John protested.

"I'll ask a few of 'em to come round," Calamity promised with a grin.

After completing the organization of the stage's defense, Calamity turned her attention once more to the Indians. She caught an approving nod from Cole in acknowledgment of her actions, which had allowed him to concentrate on keeping the enemy under observation. Neither of them offered to start shooting, wanting to conserve their ammunition until it could be put to profitable use.

Still charging recklessly at an angle down the slope, the braves must cover almost a mile of rough ground before they converged with the stagecoach on the trail. Under Pizen Joe's skilled handling the team horses ran fast and, even hauling the Concord coach, managed to build up their lead a little. Of course no harness horses could hope to out-run the Indian ponies in a long chase, especially once the latter also reached the good going of the trail. Joe knew that and intended to gain as much ground as he could. A lengthy pursuit might damp down the braves' desire for war, especially if they had more whiskey to drink.

In addition to the whiskey, the braves seemed to possess a fair number of bullets, or powder and shot. Even faced with the difficulties of riding on the slope some of them used their guns. A bullet, better aimed or luckier than the rest, passed through the coach's central window to strike the wall by Conway's head. Letting out a startled curse, he thrust himself to the window and returned the Indians' fire.

"Yield not to anger even in the face of provocation, brother," warned Cole at Conway's second ineffectual shot. "It's not the Christian way and sure wastes lead something awful."

"Why the hell don't you do something then?" snarled Conway.

"I'm doing it."

"Waiting for a miracle?"

"A miracle's what *you're* wanting, friend, cutting loose with that stingy gun at well over two hundred yards range and expecting a hit," Cole replied calmly. "I figure the Good Lord'll provide, but He expects me to help some by only shooting after I've took careful aim and at a range where I can hope to hit something."

"Hallelujah!" Calamity put in. "Which same the smoke from that fancy hip-pocket cannon's blowing right into my face, mister. It's near on blinding me and *I've* got a gun that can hit at two hundred yards, happen the target's big enough and stood still."

With an angry grunt Conway returned to his seat and glared through the window at the Indians. Yet he had to admit that Cole spoke the truth. The .31 caliber Colt Pocket Pistol revolver regardless of its name—might be ideal to carry concealed, but it could only be relied upon at close range.

Driven by a man well-versed in such matters, the coach tore along the trail at a good speed. Having passed through more than one Indian attack while on the "Bug Run," Pizen Joe knew what to expect. Already the braves were trying to shoot one of his team, knowing that to bring a horse down would fetch the coach to a sudden and disastrous halt. So far the combination of long range, hard riding, whiskey and rugged terrain prevented straight shooting, so none of the bullets had struck home. Joe realized that the closer the braves came, the better grew their chances of making a hit.

"Rock 'em a mite, Cultus!" he ordered.

Although paid good wages to fight in defense of the coach and its passengers, the guard had not yet opened fire on the Indians. Neither fear nor neglect of duty, held his hand. The Wells Fargo model shotgun was an ideal weapon for dealing with attackers at close range, but it lacked accuracy at a distance. So Cultus did not waste time or lead. Instead he served an equally important function by scooping up some of the pebbles carried in a box on the driving boot and pitching them at the rumps of the horses as an added inducement to speed. They responded once again, increasing their pace and gaining just a shade more ground.

"The dip's not far ahead," Joe reminded Cultus after a short time.

"We'll lick 'em to it," the guard replied.

"Unless there's more of 'em in it. Anyways, they'll catch up to us on the other side."

"Yep. I'd best tell the marshal."

Sliding his shotgun into his boots, Cultus leaned over the side until he hung head down at Cole's window. While he passed on the information, a bullet flung up splinters close to his suspended body and others whistled by; clear proof that the Indians drew closer.

"They've got to be showed the error of their ways," Cole decided.

"Amen to that, pastor," said Calamity, like the others having listened to Cultus' message. "Things now being where, when—and how?" She looked around at the open range. "Not out here, that's for sure."

"If we're ahead of them at the dip——," Cultus began.

"Brother, we've got to be ahead of them at it," Cole told him grimly. "You told me there's some cover on either side of the trail down there?"

"Yep."

"Enough for them to ambush us?"

"More than enough."

"Then there's plenty for us to use when we lay for them," Cole stated, not mentioning the unpleasant possibility of there being more Indians ahead.

"You mean stop the coach down the bottom——," Cultus commenced, only to be cut off before he could complete the question.

"I mean that the coach goes on and just two of us does the lying in wait," Cole answered. "Two, with rifles, ought to be enough."

"It's a chance," admitted Cultus, still retaining his uncomfortable position and ignoring the bullets which hissed through the air near him. "When do we jump?"

"*We* don't," Cole told him. "You're staying up on top ready to help fight them red devils off happen me and one of these gents don't stop 'em."

Startled expressions crossed the drummers' faces as they realized that Cole's plan called for one of them to help him. Clearly neither intended to volunteer.

"With their stingy guns?" Calamity scoffed before Cole could take the matter farther. "Because there's only two saddle-guns here and I sure as hell don't aim to loan mine to anybody."

"We need that carbine, Calam," Cole pointed out.

"Where it goes, I go," she replied. "So happen you want it out there in the dip, you'll have to take me with it."

For a long moment Cole did not reply. Studying the grim determination on Calamity's face, he knew she meant every word she said. Then his eyes went to the two drummers and still neither offered to side him in his plan. If it came to a point, Cole felt that he would not care to trust himself in a dangerous situation with either Conway or Thorbold backing him. Yelling that they would soon be at the dip, Cultus swung back to his original place. That ended the chance for lengthy discussion; which would probably have been futile anyway in the matter of making Calamity change her mind.

"Cousin Mark allowed you was ornery and stubborn as a Missouri knobhead* once you set your mind to something," Cole told her sadly.

"And he's never been righter," Calamity assured him. "You and me it is."

"Let me go," John suggested.

"You've a long and useful life ahead of you,

---

*Knobhead: A Mule.

son," Cole replied. "And anyways, I want at least *one* fighting man backing the guard should things go wrong."

"Sure, Johnny," agreed Calamity. "If things go wrong two worthless cusses like me 'n' the ma—deacon won't be missed. How's the land lie in that dip, pastor?"

Quickly Cole told her what he knew of the lie of the land and finished with, "One out of each door when we get across the stream, into the rocks and set tight until they're close enough to be hit. It'll be risky as hell, gal."

"They do say only the good die young," Calamity replied.

"There's that," Cole admitted. "So if you get shot and I don't, it ought to prove something."

Fury worked on Monique's face as she watched Calamity move across the coach to the other door. "Are you going to sit there and let a girl go outside to fight for you?" she demanded, glaring at the drummers.

"It's her carbine," Conway pointed out.

"I've got a wife and four kids back East," Thorbold continued.

"Leave 'em be, gal," Calamity advised. "It's all fixed up who's going." Then she looked at John as he sat with face working in emotion. "You know Ratchet Creek, don't you, Johnny?"

"Sure, Calam. Can't I——."

"Nope. What you *can* do is this. If something goes wrong, take my gear to ole Harry Tappet's place. Tell him what he wants's in the medicine pouch in my war bag. You'll do that for me, won't you?"

"S—Sure, Calam," John promised.

"I will help you find him, John," Monique said and directed another coldly loathing glance at the drummers.

"Thanks," Calamity replied and turned her attention to the opposite window.

Slowly the knowledge that their chances of catching up on the stage while riding along the slope sank into the whiskey-dulled minds of the Indians. First to realize it, their chief turned his horse and headed by the shortest route toward the trail. By doing so, the braves lost some ground, yet stood a better chance of regaining it with firm going under-foot. The Arapaho did not rank high among the fighting Indian tribes, which was one of the factors Cole had taken into consideration while making his plan. Nor could they claim to be as efficient horse-breeders as the Nez Perce, or Comanche nations. For all that, their ponies started to close the gap separating them from the stagecoach.

A hundred and fifty yards still separated the pursuers and pursued as the Concord approached the valley. More than once Pizen Joe heard the

eerie "Whap!" of a close-passing bullet and occasionally lead struck some part of the coach. Refus-
ing to be distracted, the old-timer concentrated on
the forthcoming descent into the dip. Normally he
would have slowed his horses to a walk, applied
the brakes and, if necessary, halted to attach the
skid chains to the wheels, then gone down in his
own good time. That could not be done with hostile Indians coming up all hot and eager to count
coup on his passengers.

"Get set inside!" he yelled as the lead horses
reached the point where the trail began its downward dip. Then he put all thoughts of the passengers' comfort right out of his mind.

As the lead pair of the team started down the
slope, Joe raised his right boot and placed it on the
brake handle. Next the swing pair went over
the edge and he started to thrust with his foot. By
the time the wheel horses followed their team-
mates on to the down-grade, the brakes began to
take effect. As the coach tilted forward, the brake-
shoes clamped on the inside of the rims and held
the rear wheels immobile. While the coach continued to move forward, it travelled too slowly to run
on to the wheel pair of horses.

A wail rose from inside the coach. Despite Joe's
warning, the sudden tipping forward took
Monique by surprise and shot her across to land
on the two drummers' laps. Calamity and John
each hooked an arm through the window and

braced their feet against the opposite seat to avoid following the French girl. Ramming his back hard against the wall of the coach, Cole watched the sides of the dip flash by.

Just before he disappeared from the Indians' sight and down the slope, Joe let out a sudden curse and jerked in his seat. Then he sank back, ignoring Cultus' question as to what caused him to do so. Sitting stiffly, the old timer watched his team galloping down the slope and approach the foot of the incline. Cultus did not trouble Joe with further questions, realizing that the next moves in the game must be timed exactly right.

On reaching the bottom, Joe must release the brake at the correct time. To leave the wheels locked would bring the coach to a halt, cause the running team to slam into its solid weight, creating confusion and possibly injury among them. Yet if he removed the restraint too soon the coach might roll forward, strike and cripple the wheel pair. Years of practical experience lay behind to help guide Joe, but he worked under an added disadvantage that his companion on the box did not suspect.

Alert to the feel of the coach, Joe watched the horses advance across the level ground. He felt the coach begin to drag as the slope's angle lessened. Only the first warning hint reached him, but it gave a message he could read. Swiftly he released the brake and the coach seemed to lurch forward faster than before. For a moment Joe wondered if his changed condition caused him to miscalculate. The coach crept slowly closer to the wheel horses and the trace straps sagged a shade more loosely than he liked. Then the wheelers drew ahead and the straps tightened without any sudden snapping that could have proved dangerous.

By this time the lead horses had drawn near to the edge of the stream. Cultus watched in concern, knowing that they might hold back from entering the water. Aware of the danger, Joe countered it. Back and out swung his whip's lash, to crack between the two leading horses' heads in a reminder of his presence. Cultus added his contribution by flicking a pebble at each horse's rump. Having made the same crossing many times without incident, the leaders did not hesitate. They felt the comforting and confident pull of the reins and plunged into the water. Obediently the swing pair followed and the wheelers added their hooves to help churn up the previously placid waters of the ford.

"Ready, Calam?" asked Cole as the coach plowed through the water.

"Ready," she agreed, turning the door handle.

They came ashore with a rush and Cole thrust open the door at his side. "Let's go then," he ordered.

Holding her carbine in both hands, Calamity sprang out of the coach. She lit down running, fighting to retain her balance on the firm gravel. At the same time she kept her eyes on the nearest large rock. Four long strides carried her to it and she dropped to her knees behind its comforting bulk. Behind her the coach started its upward climb, the horses straining against their traces and digging in the cleats of their shoes to gain a better hold on the hard surface of the trail.

"Why in hell did Wells Fargo leave these here?" Calamity mused as she settled behind the rock and considered it and others like it as potential places of concealment.

The answer was simple. When preparing the crossing-place, the Wells Fargo surveyor considered removing the rocks which offered far too convenient hiding points for anybody with evil designs on passing stagecoaches. A closer examination of the area showed that the rocks acted as a current-breaker and anchor for the ford's firm gravel bottom during times of high water. Being a shrewd young man, the surveyor raised the matter with the Company's drivers and they suggested that the rocks remained. They preferred having a reliable, safe bottom under their horses' hooves and were willing to accept the risk of an occasional hold-up to keep it.

All of which Calamity learned later. Putting

aside her thoughts about Wells Fargo's apparent
folly, which had been tinged with relief that the
Company left the rocks for her use, she prepared
for the work ahead. A look across the trail told her
that Cole was also in position, kneeling behind a
rock almost level with her. Darting a glance to the
rear, she watched the coach reach the top of the
slope. So far the Indians had not come into sight,
but the noise of their horses' hooves rumbled
nearer and the sound of shots drifted down as
they fired after the coach.

Calamity felt sweat trickle down her face and
wiped it away with her left hand. There had been
around twenty braves in the party, all apparently
armed with some kind of rifle or carbine. Only
Arapahoes maybe, but big odds against one man
and a girl. Yet two things stood in Calamity and
Cole's favor. Each of them held a fully-loaded repeater, sixteen bullets in Cole's rifle and twelve for
her carbine, and had surprise on their side.

Then the Indians appeared and began the descent into the dip in the same reckless manner
which had shown in their actions throughout the
whole affair. Every brave wished to have the
honor of counting the first coup, with its attendant
right of first choice in the sharing of the loot. So
they came down the slope in a tightly bunched
formation which might have been selected deliberately to aid Cole's plan.

Even figuring on the element of surprise, the Indians presented a mighty awe-inspiring sight to Calamity as she watched them draw closer and waited for the marshal to start the attack.

Chapter 5

STOP OTHERS DOING UNTO YOU

～◆～

"HERE THEY COME, SISTER," COLE CALLED. "LET THE first of 'em reach the foot of the slope afore we read them today's lesson."

"What's its text to be?" asked Calamity.

"Stop others doing unto you afore they get a right good chance to start doing it."

With that Cole reared into sight. The Winchester rifle swung swiftly to his shoulder and cracked viciously. An instant later Calamity's carbine spat with a lighter note, like the tenor supporting the baritone in a quartet. A vague feeling that she had forgotten something important filled the girl, but she could not spare the time to think about it as she sighted and squeezed off her first shot.

The leading buck slid sideways from his racing

pony and bounced across the gravel, a hole between his eyes. Caught in the head by a flat-nosed
.44 bullet, the second brave's mount crashed forward and somersaulted over. Its rider was the man
who had first warned Calamity of their inebriated
state by taking a drink up on the rim where she
first saw them. Drunk he might be, but a lifetime
of riding horses gave him an instinct that no
amount of liquor could dispel. Feeling his horse
collapsing under him, he tossed himself clear of it.
In landing he dropped the Springfield carbine he
carried, but kept his grip on the neck of the
whiskey jug. Carried forward by his momentum,
the buck plunged into the stream, tripped and fell
face down into the water.

Concentrating on the main body of the attackers, Calamity and Cole ignored the brave. He
thrust himself upward, spitting out water and
glared across the stream. The brief immersion
served to sober him a little. It did nothing to lessen
his desire to kill the hated white-eyes. Ignoring his
carbine, he felt around in the stream until his fingers closed on the jug's handle. Lifting the heavy
stone container, he began a cautious advance
across the stream.

In trained hands a lever-action Winchester
could throw out two bullets a second. Both
Calamity and Cole possessed the necessary skill
to take full advantage of their weapons' rate of
fire. Five more shots sped across the stream, strik-

ing down two more braves, wounding a third and tumbling yet another horse to the ground. The unexpected assault threw the remaining braves into a state of confusion that their whiskey-loaded condition did nothing to improve. Horses reared as their riders tried to halt them, sliding on the slope and crowding upon the animals before them.

As she fired her fourth shot, Calamity caught a movement from the corner of her eye. Looking closer, she saw the brave coming out of the stream. While his two-feathered hair decoration drooped and the water had washed his war paint into a smeared, running mess, he did not strike Calamity as a particularly amusing sight. Nor did the fact that all he held in his hands was a stone whiskey jug make him any the less dangerous. Unless she missed her guess, that jug would be just as deadly as a formally made war club in his hands. With that thought in mind, she flicked down the lever, felt it stick for a moment, come loose and continue its normal movement—with a slight difference.

Put simply, the carbine's breechblock was locked into the firing position by a toggle link. Lowering the lever unlocked the toggle which in turn forced back the block, ejected the empty cartridge case and left the way clear for the carrier block to rise with the next round from the magazine ready to be thrust by the returning breechblock into the chamber. In addition the back of the breechblock pushed the hammer to a firing position during its rearward movement—the innovation which put the Winchester rifle ahead of its only major competitor in the repeating stakes, for the Spencer firearms had to be thumb-cocked. Swinging up the lever reversed the procedure, the breechblock returning to its original position and leaving all ready to fire.

At least that was what should have happened, and always did on the other occasions when Calamity used her carbine. Part of the accepted sequence took place, the lever flipping back to its position under the frame; but the breechblock remained to the rear. Calamity did not need to look twice before she knew that carbine would be of no use as a firearm until repaired.

Letting out a ringing war-whoop, the Arapaho launched himself from the water in Calamity's direction. At the same moment her right hand left the carbine, flying downward—and hit the empty lip of her holster.

Suddenly, with sickening impact, Calamity recalled the reason for the nagging feeling as she took cover. She had handed her Navy Colt to young John Browning and had not troubled to ask for it back before diving from the stagecoach. To make matters worse, she did not even collect her whip and that also went off with the vehicle.

Nearer rushed the brave, swinging the whiskey jug in a way which showed his intentions plainly.

Probably the jug would be even more dangerous
in his hands than his discarded carbine at close
range. One way or another he had to be stopped,
but Calamity did not fancy trying it with her bare
hands.

Thrusting herself from behind the rock,
Calamity landed facing the Arapaho. She figured
that remaining in cover would not permit the ease
of movement the situation required. Landing on
the balls of her feet, she crouched slightly and measured the distance with her eyes. Around whirled
the whiskey jug, aimed at her head with enough
force to crush it like an eggshell. With the skill
gained in barroom brawls she jumped clear of the
jug's arc and allowed it to hiss by her harmlessly.
Before the brave could catch his balance or halt his
forward rush, he blundered by the girl. Spinning
on her heel, she swung up the Winchester and
smashed its metal-shod butt plate between his
shoulders. A howl of pain burst from the brave as
the force of the blow sent him reeling on. However
he neither dropped the jug nor went down, much
to Calamity's disappointment. Snarling Arapaho
obscenities and spitting like a gut-shot bobcat, he
brought himself to a halt and started to turn.

"Solly!" Calamity yelled as she struck the brave.
"My gun's bust!"

Already the other braves had untangled themselves and showed signs of launching a deter-
mined attack. For all that Cole did not hesitate.

One glance told him of the need for immediate action to relieve Calamity's embarrassment and he wasted no time in acting.

"Here!" he snapped and tossed the rifle.

Dropping her carbine, Calamity caught the rifle with her left hand curling around the foregrip and her right closing on the butt to slip its forefinger through the triggerguard. While taking hold, she swivelled herself around to meet the attacking brave. There was neither the time nor need for her to raise the rifle shoulder high and take careful aim. Held at hip-level, the rifle cracked in her hands. Its bullet travelled less than four feet to strike the brave's chest, Calamity thought she heard the crack of his breast bone as the bullet arrived. Jerking backward, he spun around, let the jug drop from his fingers and measured his length on the gravel.

After tossing his rifle to Calamity, Cole's left hand swooped down to the Rogers & Spencer's butt. Drawing from such a holster as he wore took a different technique from that employed on the more conventional rig. Instead of lifting the gun so its barrel cleared the lip of the holster, he pivoted it forward from the grip of the retaining spring and downward until the muzzle left the slot in the bottom plug. Then he swung it up smoothly to point in the required direction. As he drew, Cole went into the gun-fighter's crouch. From waist high, with the revolver held centrally in the rectangle of his body, using instinctive alignment instead of taking sight, Cole turned his first bullet loose slightly less than a second after beginning his draw. Lead ripped into the body of the nearest brave and he splashed down into the stream.

Levering another bullet into the rifle's chamber, Calamity turned and cradled the butt against her shoulder. Although it was some four inches longer and two pounds heavier than the carbine, she found no difficulty in handling the rifle. Carbine and rifle had been designed to take the same type of bullet and, if anything, the extra weight of the latter tended to ease the recoil kick. Besides which, Calamity had no desire to make super-accurate shots, like an Eastern sportsman popping holes in a paper target at long range. She merely took rough sight along the barrel at the nearest Indian and did not care where she hit him, figuring that two hundred grains of carefully shaped lead ought to take at least some of the fight out of him when it drove home.

Guns spoke from the slope behind Calamity and Cole. The deep, authoritative boom of a ten-gauge shotgun almost drowned the lighter note of a Navy Colt which in turn helped to swamp an even more pip-squeak crack. Yet another brave made an involuntary dismount as nine .34 caliber buckshot balls slashed among the attackers. However he struggled to his feet and swung aboard a companion's pony.

Already demoralized by the unexpected reversal to their plans, discouraged by the losses inflicted on them by Calamity and Cole, the remaining Arapahoes called off their attack. Swinging their horses, gathering up the wounded in passing, they plunged back across the water through which they had charged so boldly. Calamity and Cole held their fire, watching the retreat. Although the shotgun and Navy Colt also fell silent, the lighter revolver sounded twice more but there was no noticeable effect on the fleeing braves.

After watching to make sure that none of the braves turned back in a final attempt at revenge, Cole swung about. He looked up the slope to where John Browning, Cultus and Conway approached with guns in their hands.

"I thought I told you to get the coach to safety," the marshal said.

"Was going to," Cultus replied. "Then I recalled that we never stopped to scout the draw afore coming over. So ole Joe hauled up and told us to come back and do it."

"Right pleased to see you," Calamity stated and went to pick up her carbine. "You come just at the right time."

"You're saying the truth, sister," Cole agreed,

holstering his revolver and going to pick up the whiskey jug.

"If there's anything in it, save me one," Calamity said. "I can sure—."

Her words cut off as a scared female scream rang out from beyond the rim where the stagecoach had halted. Swiftly the party bounded up the trail, Cole carrying the jug and Calamity encumbered by the two Winchesters. None of them knew what to expect to see when they reached the top.

At first sign there did not seem any reason for the scream. The coach had halted about a hundred yards beyond the rim and Thorbold stood by the heads of the lead horses. Then Calamity and the men saw Monique kneeling alongside Pizen Joe as he lay sprawled on his back.

"He just got off the box and dropped," Thorbold told them as they ran up. "Let me get to him!" Calamity snapped, then realized that she still carried her own carbine and Cole's rifle. "And will somebody lay hold of all this hardware? I feel like the gun counter at Milligan's store."

"Let me have them, Calam," offered Johnny and thrust her Colt back into its holster to leave both hands free.

"Thanks," she said, surrendering the Winchesters and going to kneel at the old-timer's side. To her relief, she saw his eyes flicker open. "What the hell're you doing down here, you fool ole goat."

"I'm taking me aftynoon nap, what else?" Joe yelped and struggled to sit up. "Just let me——."

Pain twisted his face and sweat burst on his face, causing him to flop back into a lying position again.

"That's better," Calamity told him. "Now stay there or I'll have the boys sit on your chest."

Gently she slipped a hand under his neck and started to ease him from the ground. A gasp broke from him as Calamity moved her hand downward to support his back. Something hot, wet, sticky and familiar to the touch came into contact with her palm. She looked down at a blood-oozing hole beneath his right shoulder blade.

"God damn it, Joe!" she said. "You've been shot."

"Now me, I'd've swore some damned fool freighter done stuck me out of meanness with a pitchfork," the old timer replied hotly. "Course I've been shot. Lend me hand up, one of ye, and we'll be on our way."

"Like hell!" Calamity barked. "You're bad enough driving well. The Good Lord only knows what you'd be like with a bullet in you."

"Damn it all, gal!" Joe spluttered indignantly. "I druv the 'Big Run' from Halleck to Bridger one time with three Sioux arrers in me brisket. Leave be——."

Seeing that strong measures were called for to

obtain the old timer's cooperation, Calamity bent forward and hissed words that reached only his ears. "If you don't get shut and lie still I'll tell everybody I meet that those five damned scalps're nothing but the pullings from hosses' tails."

"How'd you know about that?" Joe demanded, concern and contrition warring with the agony on his face.

"Never you mind. But I *do* know."

"Dobe Killem warned me that you was a real mean cuss and got a plumb ornery streak, gal," Joe complained. "I bet you would tell on me at that."

A slight grin twisted at Calamity's lips, and she could imagine her boss saying it. Knowing that Dobe Killem suffered with "Cecil" as a Christian name came in useful on such occasions as when their wills clashed on some issue. So she figured a similar form of blackmail ought to stifle Joe's protests and make him see reason.

"Spread a tarp on the ground some of you," she said to the watching men. "Then come and help ease him on to it. Johnny, go up the top and throw down my bedroll."

"This's a whole heap of fuss for nothing!" Joe growled. "I'm not hurt bad."

And saying it he collapsed unconscious in Calamity's arms.

"You're an awful old liar, Joe, but you've got more guts than they could hang on the biggest corral's fence," the girl said quietly, thinking of the courage needed to continue driving with such a wound. "When'd this happen?"

"It must've been as we started into the dip," Cultus replied. "He gave a jump like he'd been bee-stung just afore we went over."

"You mean he took us through there at that speed with a bullet in him?" Conway gulped.

"He for sure d——," Cultus began.

"Next fall'll do fine for me to get that tarp spread!" Calamity interrupted coldly. "Only it snows something fierce up this way then and I don't reckon Joe can wait that long."

Goaded into movement by Calamity's cold voice, the men prepared to obey her orders. John shinned up the side of the coach to reach its roof, unfastened the tarpaulin cover and exposed the passengers' baggage. In his haste to collect Calamity's bedroll, he tangled it with his carpet bag and tipped the latter over the side. Monique gave a startled squeak as the bag thudded down at her feet and hopped hurriedly aside, drawing the others' attention to her. Not that they looked for long at her, but turned their eyes to the ground. In landing, the carpet-bag burst open and scattered its contents on the ground. A clean shirt, change of underclothing and roll of toilet articles bounced into view, closely followed by a bulky oblong leather case. None of the items, even the case, were sufficiently out of the ordinary

to warrant the amount of interest shown by the
onlookers.

The two thick pads of money which accompanied the other items into sight formed the source
of attraction.

A low whistle broke from Conway. Thorbold
stared with eyes bugged out like organ-stops. Letting out a soft gasp, Monique darted a glance at
the others. Calamity and Cole exchanged aston-
ished looks. Only Cultus remained unaffected.
During his time riding shotgun for Wells Fargo he
had seen so many curious items among passengers' baggage that the sight of the money failed to
arouse his interest.

With Calamity's bedroll clutched in his hand,
John dropped from the top of the coach. Despite
there being one thousand dollars of his father's
hard-earned savings lying in plain view, he
showed little concern as he went to the girl.

"That's a whole heap of cash for a young feller
to be toting," Cole said.

"It's to pay for the machinery, sir," John explained. "We've only just managed to save enough
to buy it."

"Was I you, I'd find a better place to carry it than
that," Calamity told him as she took the bedroll.

"Shucks, no owlhoot'd expect a kid my age to be
carrying this much," John objected, gathering his
belongings. "The last place they'd think of looking's in my bag."

"Or the first," Calamity said dryly. "What's up now?"

John raised his eyes from examining the money. "There's blood-stains on the top bills of each bundle," he replied. "Must've got there when I looked inside after the fight in Promontory. I sure hope that doesn't stop the money being good."

"I can't see why it should," Calamity answered and glared at the other passengers. "Let's have the tarp spread, shall we?"

"Come on, brother," Cole told the guard. "Get it out."

Producing a spare sheet of tarpaulin from the rear boot, Cultus opened it out and laid it upon the ground. Then the other men raised and carried Pizen Joe's limp body and laid it down. Calamity eyed the men with disfavor as she slid the old timer's bowie knife from its sheath.

"Reckon I can work without getting hip-deep in war-whoops?"

"They'll not be back," Cultus replied.

"Did they write and tell you so, or send up smoke-signals?" Calamity growled. "They didn't look that obliging to me."

"Go watch the gap, brother," suggested Cole. "Likely those bucks've had a belly-full, but I'd sooner be sure than sorry."

"I reckon I would sooner know they're about by seeing than by picking their arrers out of my ribs," admitted Cultus. "Come on, Johnny boy. Two can keep a better watch than one."

"You could tote along my carbine, but the damned thing's bust on me," Calamity remarked as she cut away the old timer's shirt.

"Take my rifle, boy," Cole ordered. "And you gents go out one on each side of a piece to watch in case those red varmints've found another crossing."

"Says which?" growled Conway.

"Says me, *hombre*," Cole replied quietly, yet his voice had taken on a new and harder note. "So go to it right away—and *pronto*."

New from the East, Conway knew only vaguely about Utah Territory's U.S. marshal and did not connect Cole with that important post. Nor had the drummer been present during the trouble in Promontory, where he would have learned Cole's identity. Although regarding the marshal as no more than a mighty unconventional preacher, Conway felt disinclined to argue with him. Recalling how the other acted all through the Indian attack, he concluded objections would be unwise.

"We don't have rifles," Thorbold protested feebly.

"All you have to do is watch," Cole answered. "That and get back here fast at the first sign of trouble."

"One thing you yahoos best get into your fool heads," Calamity put in. "That coach can't go without a driver, which's either Joe or me. He can't do it and I don't aim to until I've patched up his ornery, worthless old hide. So you pair'd best do just what the ma—deacon says. Go keep watch and leave me to my work."

Chapter 6

OLD JOE'LL BUST A GUT

CALAMITY'S WARNING ADDED THE DECIDING NOTE TO the argument. Muttering to themselves, the two drummers went sullenly to stand watch on the rims flanking the stagecoach. Putting all thoughts of them out of her mind, she prepared to start her work on the wounded old timer.

"Do you want to help me, honey?" Calamity asked Monique.

A startled expression crossed the girl's face and she took a hurried pace to the rear. "*Non*! No!" she gasped.

"Can't say as how I blame you. Say, I bet you've got some of them fancy white do-dads on underneath. Get in the coach and toss a couple out."

"I don't——," Monique began.

"For bandages, sister," Calamity elaborated. "I'd look like hell wearing 'em over my pants."

"Of course!" Monique replied, hands fluttering to her skirt's waistband. "I didn't think for the moment."

With that she turned and disappeared into the coach. Nodding in satisfaction, Calamity continued her interrupted removal of the driver's shirt. Needing help, she looked up in search of the marshal and felt a mite surprised at his occupation.

After the departure of the drummers, Cole had picked up the jug he had collected at the river so as to enforce his demands if necessary. Slowly he turned it in his hands, studying it with far more care and interest than such a commonplace object appeared to merit. In particular he gazed at the maker's name and a number painted on the side in prominent black figures. Then he tilted the jug and looked at its bottom.

"This's no time to start thinking about taking a quick snort, deacon," Calamity remarked.

"Huh?" grunted Cole. "What'd you say, Calam?"

There was something changed in his attitude. The solemn expression had been replaced by a cold, grim mask that told Calamity of the true man behind his pose. However she was in no mood to worry about minor details.

"Lend me a hand here, will you," she said.

"Sure, sister," he agreed and the old way came

back to him. "Let me just put this some place safe."

Calamity felt puzzled by Cole's interest in the jug, although she could see the reason for it. Selling liquor to Indians had long been a crime of Federal as well as local interest. Naturally Cole wanted to know who put the fluid dynamite in the hands of the Arapahoes. For all that, Calamity failed to see what he hoped to learn from the type of jug used by almost every whiskey distiller in the West. She put the thought out of her mind as the sound of ripping reached her ears and several strips of white cloth were hung on the window of the coach.

After examining the wound closely, Calamity decided against trying to remove the bullet. So she contented herself with making sure no more blood flowed and then bandaged Joe's torso.

"That's about all I can do for him right now," she told Cole. "Let's get him someplace where a doctor can take a look at it."

"I'd say go on to Coon Hollow way station," Cole suggested. "We can send a telegraph message to Promontory and have a doctor ride out."

"It'll be quicker that way," Calamity admitted. "'Sides which, those Arapahoes might be on the trail back that ways."

"I'll ask for an escort to side the doctor," Cole promised. "Let's get the others in and see about loading Joe aboard."

"Sure," Calamity replied. "I want to be moving."

"When you go, sister," Cole told her. "Let your driving be like that of Jehu, son of Nimshi, for he went like a bat out of hell."

Calamity eyed the sober face, with its twinkling eyes and grinned. "Some of your pards have real fancy names."

On hearing Cole's shout, the lookouts returned, Conway and Thorbold showing considerable relief at being recalled with their scalps intact. Under Calamity's profane guidance, the men lifted Joe and carried him to the coach. They placed the old timer on the forward seat and Cultus produced some straps which could be used to hold Joe in position. Leaving the coach, Calamity saw Cole at the rear boot. On joining him, she found that he stood placing the whiskey jug in his capacious travelling bag.

"You wanting it for evidence?" she asked.

"Sure."

"It looks just like any other whiskey jug to me."

"Looks that way to most folks," Cole said cryptically. "Let's go."

Something in the marshal's attitude warned Calamity that he did not intend to discuss the matter. So she returned to the door and looked into the coach. Monique was perched on the seat alongside Joe and the men sat facing her. Satisfied that nothing more could be done—John had taken the Winchesters inside and placed them on the racks—Calamity climbed to the driving box.

"Riding up top here, Calam?" Cultus inquired innocently.

"Yep."

"Want the loan of my shotgun?"

"I'd sooner use a whip."

"Are you aiming to *drive*?" Cultus asked in well-stimulated surprise.

"I sure as hell am!" Calamity answered. "Riding behind that wored-out ole goat's bad enough and he's a fair driver—as Wells Fargo drivers go—but I'm not risking my dainty lil neck with you handling the ribbons."

Having made her point, Calamity paused and looked around her. Under the seat rested a heavily-padlocked Wells Fargo "treasure chest" with the Company's stiff-backed official Driver's Delivery Receipt book on its lid. A quartet of U.S. Mail sacks, also padlocked, occupied the remaining space beneath the seat.

"We're carrying five thousand dollars for the Ratchet Creek bank," Cultus explained, following the direction of her gaze.

"Is that why the marshal's along?"

"Not that I know of. It was a last-minute arrangement sprung on us in Promontory. We didn't even have time to fix for another messenger to ride inside."

Knowing that "messenger" used in such a manner meant a guard, Calamity nodded her understanding. She knew the strict precautions Wells

Fargo took to protect its often valuable shipments and did not doubt that the consignment for the Ratchet Creek bank had been kept a secret. One thing was for sure. She could not sit on top of the motionless stagecoach and worry about the possibility of a hold-up. So she sank down on to the seat and immediately jerked up slightly. Her right hand shot under her rump to poke at the seat's cover.

"Well dog-my-cats if the ole goat hasn't got a feather cushion under here!"

"The hell you say!" ejaculated Cultus and reached to check her statement.

"Get your cotton-picking hand off!" ordered Calamity, flicking it away. "Us drivers like our comforts."

With that she sat down and studied the situation. First thing to strike her was the difference in height between the stagecoach's driving seat and the box of her wagon. She seemed to be way up in the air and wondered how it would affect her judgment.

Although her whip once more rode in its usual place at her side, she drew Joe's from its holder at the side of the boot. It proved to be an entirely different pattern to that developed by freight-wagon drivers and felt awkward in her hand, despite being the same overall length as her own. Gripping the six-foot long handle, she tried a couple of experimental flicks and found she could not control the lash with any degree of accuracy.

"I reckon I'd best use my own," she remarked.

Hoping she looked a whole heap more confident than she felt, Calamity then unfastened the reins and gripped them between her fingers. She blessed the good fortune which had caused Dobe Killem to adopt the same system as Wells Fargo, instead of following the trend of having the driver ride the near wheel horse and guide the lead pair by means of a single rein. Normally Calamity was not a girl troubled by self-doubts, but she paused for a moment and sucked in a long breath before she slid free her whip and shook loose its lash.

"Giddap!" she snapped and cracked the whip in the air.

Instantly the horses moved forward, thrusting into their harness. Calamity felt life run through the reins and deftly checked any undue enthusiasm the team were inclined to show at moving off after a rest. Although the coach did not make quite the smooth start that Joe could manage, Calamity felt she might have done far worse.

There were differences, obviously, between handling a heavy freight wagon and driving the light stagecoach, but Calamity rapidly gained the feel of her new vehicle. At her side, Cultus watched with at first concern, then admiration. However he remained silent for a time, figuring that she needed to concentrate. It never occurred to him that he might advise the girl about the horses' individual characteristics. Anybody claiming to be a driver would take offense at such a liberty, being full capable of forming his, or her, own conclusions.

Tense and alert, Calamity concentrated on her work. The height she sat above the ground tended at first to confuse her, but she quickly became used to it. Although she soon grew accustomed to the difference in weights, and found the Concord coach handled like the thoroughbred it was, she did not relax and grow careless.

At last Cultus felt he should give a warning. "Best hold down on the speed a mite, Calam. We've a lot of miles to cover."

"I'm going too fast, huh?"

"Just a lil mite."

"It's hard to tell, she rides so smooth."

"Shucks, you're no worse'n old Joe," Cultus informed her with a grin. "I mind one time we reached Ratchet Creek the day afore we left Promontory."

Fortunately during the early part of the drive, the stagecoach trail ran straight and over level ground. By the time they reached the first curve, Calamity knew enough about the Concord's handling qualities to take it around without difficulty. Then they started to climb a hill. Although Calamity noticed that the coach made the ascent with greater ease than her wagon would have, she knew going down might be more tricky.

So it proved. Used to the need to exert considerable force to operate her wagon's brakes, Calamity gave the handle a hard shove with her foot. Immediately she saw her mistake and drew back her leg just a shade too quickly. Disaster might have resulted, but for the fact that an experienced team pulled the coach. Feeling the sudden jolt caused by the application of the brakes, then the slackening of the traces caused by their removal, the horses increased their speed in order to avoid being run down. Cursing savagely, Calamity made a more tentative try at controlling the speed.

"What the hell's she doing?" Conway snarled as the coach jolted and rocked.

"Her best, brother," Cole answered. "Which nobody can do better."

"You're doing good, Calam," Cultus said as they reached the bottom of the slope.

"I'm doing lousy," she replied. "But don't tell me so."

"Not while you're toting the whip," he grinned, and let her concentrate on the driving once more.

Backed by almost three years experience of handling a six-horse team, Calamity rapidly mastered the different techniques involved in driving the stagecoach. At her side, Cultus nodded approvingly on reaching the bottom of the next slope. He had to admit that she had made no glaring mistake and had brought down the coach almost as well as Pizen Joe would have done it. Settling back in his seat, Cultus put aside his doubts and misgivings. Maybe all the stories he had heard about Calamity Jane were not true, but she could sure drive.

Time went by and Calamity reached the stage where she did not need to devote all her attention to the work at hand.

"Wonder how Joe is?" she said.

"I don't know how he is right now," admitted Cultus with a chuckle. "But I sure know how he's going to be."

"How?"

"Mad as a razorback hawg that's backed into a still-fire. Ole Joe'll bust a gut when he knows you're up top."

"Reckon he won't trust me?"

"Calam," Cultus replied. "He don't even trust other Wells Fargo drivers to handle his rig. See them trees over there?"

"Sure."

"We allus make our long stop there something like them Arapahoes show to stop us."

"Can't see anybody after us now," Calamity remarked without turning.

On arrival at the trees Calamity brought the coach to a halt. She heard a weak wail of anguish rise from inside and looked at Cultus. "What's that?"

"I'd say ole Joe's just woke up and learned what's happening," he answered. "Long stop, folks. Light and rest yourselves."

"Can I help you, Calamity?" John asked, jumping down.

"I thought you'd never ask," she smiled and glanced at Cultus who stood at the open door. "Hey, can we trust these wind-broke ole 'navvies' not to cut loose and run when we loose 'em?"

"If you tie their tails together," the guard replied over a spluttering burst of curses from within the coach. Joining the girl, he dropped his voice and continued, "You've done real good on the old timer, Calam. He sounds better already."

"Them as don't die when I fix 'em mostly do," Calamity answered. "I'll be happier when a doctor's seen him, though." She went to the door and looked in. "Hey, Joe, how's things?"

Twisting his head, Pizen Joe scowled at the girl. Under its tan, the leathery old face looked pale, and pain twisted at it. For all that, he managed a glare and his voice held something of its normal note as he replied, "You bust up my——."

"Ah, shut up!" Calamity interrupted coarsely and winked at Monique who sat alongside the old timer. "Most fellers'd enjoy being laid there with a right pretty gal nursing 'em. 'Course, you're getting too old for that."

"Old?" Joe spluttered. "I'll——."

"Some of us have work to do," Calamity told him. "Don't go away."

Turning before the old timer could think up a reply—one suitable to be used with Monique at his side—Calamity walked away. Already Cultus and John had begun to unhitch the team and she joined them. Once liberated, each horse enjoyed a good roll on the grass and Calamity checked them for signs of harness chafing. She did not expect to find any, but figured Joe would want her to exercise the same care as she showed to her own team. While her helpers led the horses to drink at a stream close by, Calamity took the nosebags from the rear boot and made up feeds in them.

When the horses returned, Calamity supervised the feeding. Although she did not offer any advice to John, she watched him to make sure he fitted the nosebags correctly. Clearly John had worked with horses enough to be aware that a loose, low hanging nosebag made trouble. In order to reach the food at the bottom, when the bag hung slackly, the horse would toss its head and spill a fair amount of the contents. Aware of that, and wanting to make a good impression on the girl, John buckled each nose-bag as high as it would go.

Calamity's work kept her too busy at first to allow her to bother with the other passengers. As she helped John to fit the last nosebag into place, her attention wandered a little. Everything seemed to be going smoothly, with the travellers making the most of the halt. Marshal Cole sat with his back against the coach's rear off wheel, holding the upturned whiskey jug between his knees as he scraped at its bottom with the blade of a knife. Standing some distance away from Cole, Conway and Thorbold conversed in low tones. As Calamity glanced their way, Conway was showing Thorbold something and both looked at John. Seeing the girl's eyes on them, Conway whipped his extended hand into his pocket. If the man had not done so, Calamity would have thought nothing of the incident. His sudden movement caused her to look closely and she identified the object he clearly wished to avoid her seeing as a deck of cards. From inside the coach came the sound of Monique's voice as she gave Joe a report of Calamity's progress.

"Damned if the ole goat don't expect me to slit those fool hosses' throats, or bust a couple of wheels," she grinned. "Have you anything to eat, Johnny?"

"Ma put me some up, but——," John began.

"You ate it all," she finished for him. "Come on, I've some pemmican that we can share."

Collecting her bedroll from the top of the coach, Calamity opened it. Inside her warbag, wrapped in a piece of clean cloth, was a roll of "Indian bread," pemmican.* Exposing the roll, Calamity borrowed Pizen Joe's bowie knife and carved off two liberal slices of the range-country delicacy.

"What tribe made this?" Johnny asked, after munching off a couple of hefty mouthfuls.

"He allows to be Cantonese, or some such," Calamity answered with a grin.

"I never heard of that tribe before. Are they one of the Sioux bands?"

"Nope. Chinese. Our outfit's cook makes it as good as any Indian."

"You can say that again," Johnny told her enthusiastically.

While Calamity replaced the depleted pemmican, John entered the coach and returned holding her carbine. The girl gave him permission to examine it, but had sufficient faith in him not to add any warnings. Any boy reared in the frontier learned early to treat firearms with respect and not to regard them as toys. That ought to apply with extra force to a son of Jonathan Browning, gunsmith.

Her faith was not misplaced, for Johnny held the barrel directed upward and pointing away from the other passengers. Sitting down, he rested the little gun on his knees and worked its lever a couple of times in a thoughtful way.

---

*A recipe for making pemmican is given in COMANCHE.

"Well," Calamity said, watching him. "What's wrong with it."

Although she did not expect a reply, John gave one immediately. "The toggle links have come apart, I'd say."

"Can I get them fixed?"

"Sure. It's not a hard job."

Before they could say any more, Cole walked over to join them. He no longer held the jug and looked his usual solemn self.

"How soon'll you be moving, Calam?"

"Not long now. Are you in a hurry?"

"You might say that."

"We'd best think about shifting then," Calamity stated. "Put the carbine in the coach, Johnny and let's start work again."

"Yes'm," John replied. He seemed on the verge of saying something more but thought better of it. Carrying the carbine into the coach, he returned it to its place on the wall. Turning, he found a worried Monique looking at him.

"Tell Calamity," she said, "I think Joe is getting worse."

John passed on the message and Calamity came fast. Swinging into the coach, she looked down at the old man. No longer did he lie looking about him and muttering faint complaints at the need to be kept in such a position. Instead he lay unmoving, sweat soaking his face and breathing so shal-

low that it barely made any movement of his chest.
One glance told Calamity all she needed to know.

"That bullet's going to have to come out!" she
breathed.

"Here?" gulped Monique.

"Nope. At Coon Hollow way station. Maybe
there'll be somebody on hand who can do it."

"And if there isn't?"

For a long moment Calamity did not reply.
Sucking in a long breath, she looked at the old
timer, then raised her eyes to Monique's face.

"Then I'll have to do it myself."

And, if the worst came to the worst, Calamity
figured that Pizen Joe would want to die under a
roof, with his boots off and in bed.

Chapter 7

I WISH YOU WAS A DOCTOR

CoON HOLLOW WAY STATION HAD BEEN ERECTED BY
the Wells Fargo Company at a sufficient distance
from Promontory to present stagecoaches en route
to Rachet Creek with a convenient place for a
night halt. So far it had not attracted residents
other than Company employees and their fami-
lies, although situated in a pleasant location close
to a small lake. In time other people might settle in
the vicinity, building a hamlet and, if fortune
smiled, even expand into a prosperous town.
Other communities rose along the tendrils of the
Wells Fargo and other stagecoach trails in such
manner.

Two large pole corrals and a sizeable stables

housed livestock for use by the Company's various enterprises, for Wells Fargo did not deal exclusively with mail and passengers travelling by stagecoach. A couple of small log cabins accommodated the agent's assistants, while he and his family lived in the big main building. Set up strongly enough to act as a fort in time of need, this latter consisted of a bar and diningroom, kitchen, bedrooms, office and the agent's quarters. It offered the passengers adequate facilities to spend a comfortable night while travelling.

Night had fallen as Calamity brought the coach down the trail toward the buildings and they made a mighty welcome sight for the girl. During the last part of the journey Joe's condition grew gradually worse. Yet there was nothing she could do for him on the trail. So she pushed on grimly, driving the horses as fast as she dared and taking chances in her inexperience with the coach. Never had anything been so welcome to her eyes as the glowing light of the way station's windows. She prayed silently that help would be on hand.

Surprise showed on the agent's face as he stood on the porch of the main building and watched the approaching coach. Although he could not identify Calamity as a woman, he knew that Pizen Joe did not handle the ribbons. In a casual manner he dropped his right hand to the revolver in his waistband.

"Hey, Curly!" Cultus yelled, seeing the move and knowing that the agent was taking precautions against a surprise attack. "Joe's inside. He's been shot and's hurt real bad."

Immediately the burly, bald agent removed his hand. He knew that Cultus would not be riding the box or acting in such a manner unless the driver could be trusted. Walking forward, he saw the coach's door open and a man swing out.

"Is your telegraph working?" Solly Cole demanded before the agent could form any idea as to the reason for his appearance.

The suspicions which sprang to the agent's mind died as he saw the open wallet in Cole's hand. From the way the marshal's badge was shown, the agent concluded that he did not wish his official status disclosed to the other passengers. A U.S. marshal's wishes on any matter were better respected, so Agent Janowska nodded his agreement.

"Sure it is. I'll be with you as soon——."

"Go now, mister," Calamity put in, already off the box and headed for the coach's door. "Get word to the nearest doctor."

"I have to check in the treas——," Janowska began.

"Go send the message, Curly!" Cultus interrupted. "I'll see that nobody steals the chest or mail afore you get back."

Although a way station's agent might rank

higher than a shot-gun-messenger in the Company's hierarchy, Janowska did not press the point of seniority. One look at Cultus' grim face warned him that the guard did not intend allowing even the safety of the "treasure chest" and mail bags to delay sending for medical aid. So Janowska put aside all thoughts of waiting until after they had been locked in his office's safe.

"Sure, Cultus," he said, darting curious glances at Calamity. "I'll get to it right away."

"I'll come with you, brother," Cole told him and looked at the two drummers as they prepared to leave the coach by its other door. "I reckon you two gents'll not mind lending a hand with Pizen Joe?"

"Naw, we'll help out," Conway replied although he did not look too pleased with the idea.

"There's nobody here knows about doctoring, is there?" Calamity inquired from inside the coach.

"Only my wife," Janowska answered. "Come in—I'll shout for her."

Under Calamity's guidance, Cultus, the drummers and one of the agent's men removed Joe's still body from the coach to carry him into the building. Already on hand, Mrs. Janowska put off until later her routine work of welcoming the guests and allocating sleeping quarters. She asked no questions, but led the way to one of the doors at the rear of the big combined bar and diningroom. After carrying Joe into the room and setting him down on the bed, the drummers made a hurried departure. Cultus and the other Wells Fargo employee remained, hovering in the background as the woman stood alongside the old timer.

"You'd best go tend to the team and that damned box," Calamity told them.

"Sure, Calam," Cultus replied.

As the two men left, John put his head around the door. "Can I help, Calam?" he asked.

"No!" she snapped and immediately regretted sounding so brusque. Drawing back, he closed the door before she could think up an apology.

Already Janowska was sitting at the table in the telegraph office where he rattled out a request for a doctor to be sent from Promontory, adding a warning about the Arapahoes and suggesting that an armed escort accompany him. While the agent worked, Cole wrote out a message for his office in Promontory. Reading Cole's writing, Janowska wondered what the cryptic message meant. He asked no questions but once again started the key moving to flash the marshal's words to the waiting operator at the other end.

"Will it be delivered tonight?" Cole inquired to Janowska stopped using the telegraph key.

"If they can find the feller it's sent to."

"He'll be around, or I'll want to know why when I get back. Let me know the answer as soon as it comes through."

"Sure, marshal."

Leaving the telegraph room, Cole paused to study the situation. By the front door Monique stood watching the men carry in the "treasure chest" and mail bags. John Browning walked by them and outside, looking a mite put out, or Cole missed his guess. By the bar, Conway and Thorbold took drinks served by a grizzled old man. Cole ignored them as he crossed the room and asked where Joe had been taken. On learning, he went to the room and entered.

"It's bad, marshal," Calamity announced in a quiet voice. "That bullet's got to come out right soon."

"I hope you're a doing man, as well as a praying man, deacon," Mrs. Janowska went on. "I've never taken a bullet out of a man."

"Or me," Cole told her.

"Which makes three of us," Calamity concluded. "Well, there's got to be a first time for everything they do say. Let's make a start of it."

"You'll need hot water, bandages——," Mrs. Janowska began.

"And a knife," Calamity went on. "Something a mite handier than that damned great toad-stabber Joe totes."

"See if you can raise something to feel down for the bullet with, ma'am," Cole finished.

"I'll get them," the woman promised and hurried from the room.

"Marshal," Calamity said quietly. "I wish you was a doctor, or a real parson, or I was a hundred miles from here——."

"You'll do fine, Calam," Cole replied gently. "Cousin Mark allowed you're a good gal to have around in a calamity."

"Ole Mark said that about *me*?"

"Why he always talks highly of you—sometimes."

"Say, why in hell do you make out like you're a preacher?" Calamity asked, as much to take her mind off what lay ahead as to satisfy her curiosity.

"Got like it working for the U.S. Secret Service just after the War, hunting counterfeiters——."

"What in hell're they?"

"Forgers, they make their own money. Well, there was one of 'em called the Deacon. Real smart jasper too, but he made a mistake and Belle Boyd got on his trail—."

"Belle Boyd, the Rebel Spy?"*

"Sure. She was like me, went to work for the Yankee Secret Service when the War ended. Anyways, the Deacon got word we were after him and——."

It seemed that Cole's explanation was doomed to be interrupted. Mrs. Janowska entered, carrying a bottle of whiskey and a steaming kettle. Set-

*Belle Boyd's story is told in THE COLT AND THE SABRE and THE REBEL SPY.

ting them down by the bed, she took a long, thin carving knife and a meat-skewer from her apron's pocket.

"I'll fetch the bandages now," she said.

An Eastern surgeon might have thrown up his hands in horror if asked to perform an operation with such meager and unusual equipment, but the items which Mrs. Janowska brought were all that stood between Pizen Joe and death.

"Let's get at it," Calamity suggested in the kind of tone used when faced with an unpleasant but necessary task.

In a land of sparsely populated and vast distances most people picked up at least a rudimentary knowledge of medical and surgical skill. Both Calamity and Cole had seen bullets removed and so possessed some idea of what to do. Hygiene and sterilization were at that time novel ideas even in the major hospitals of the East, while evening dews and damps were among the other things believed to cause lockjaw, gangrene or septicemia. So Calamity and Cole did no more than soak their collection of instruments in whiskey and run them through the flame of matches. Then the girl took the skewer and walked purposefully toward the bed.

On the porch of the main building, young John Browning stood glaring into the darkness. He had wanted to help Calamity, but she had refused his offer in a way which hurt his feelings. At that moment John, feeling the first pangs of puppy-love, suffered like all rejected lovers.

"Hey, Johnny," Cultus called. "How about toting Calamity and the marshal's gear inside for us?"

For a moment the boy felt like telling him to throw Calamity's gear into the lake. Then he realized the kind of strain she must be under and relented. Going to the side of the coach, he caught his carpetbag and Calamity's bedroll as the guard dropped them down. Next he collected the two Winchesters from inside and gathered Cole's bag from the boot. Well loaded, he entered the building and set his burden down on the table.

At which point John remembered about Calamity's carbine being broken. There was a way to impress her with his ability and knowledge. If he mended it, she would see him in a far better light and regard him as something more than a village kid who needed watching over. With that thought in mind, he opened his bag and took out the bulky leather wallet.

Bringing the other passengers' baggage in, Cultus saw John with the open bag and remembered what it held. "Why not put that money in the safe until morning, Johnny?" he asked.

Normally John was a sensible and level-headed youngster—he later proved to be a much shrewder businessman than his over-generous father—but at that moment he suffered from the pangs of his first love, a condition noted for making one act foolishly. Born and raised in a small Mormon community made him a touch naive in such matters, but he felt sure that Calamity would have no respect for a man who needed someone else to safeguard his property. So he shook his head firmly.

"No, it'll be safe enough."

"Have it your own way," Cultus said and went to attend to his business.

A pretty girl of John's age entered the room from the kitchen, carrying a tray with steaming coffeepot, milk jug, sugar basin, cups and biscuits on it. Telling the passengers that supper would be ready in half an hour, she darted an interested glance in the youngster's direction. He ignored her, being more concerned with his plans to win Calamity's approbation.

Clearing the top of the table, he laid the carbine on it and opened the wallet. Inside lay several tools and a selection of the spare parts a gunsmith found himself most likely to need: main-springs—which propelled the hammer against the charge's percussion cap—for Colt, Smith & Wesson or Remington revolvers, Winchester and Sharps rifles, firing pins for the Henry and other cartridge rifles and sets of toggle links. Made up for him by his father, the wallet offered John all he required to perform the repair and so earn Calamity's gratitude and, he hoped, affection.

While John might labor under a feeling of unrequited love, he did not allow it to override good sense where his work was concerned. If his diagnosis of the trouble was correct, and he did not doubt it would be, making the repair posed no great problem. First, however, he must take the basic precaution of unloading the carbine. Doing so the usual way meant operating the lever and ejecting the bullets in the manner of its empty cases. With the breechblock inoperative that would not be possible.

After ensuring that the muzzle pointed at the outside wall, John selected a screwdriver and began to unfasten the side plate of the frame. With the mechanism exposed, he saw that he had guessed correctly as to the cause of the trouble. His first concern was to render the carbine harmless. Carefully easing back the breechblock, which he had closed before taking it into the stagecoach, he let the bullet slip out of the chamber. Then he held down the carrier block and tipped the remaining rounds from the magazine tube. Not until he was sure that he need not fear an accidental discharge did he start work.

Such was the simplicity of the Winchester's mechanism that John changed its most important operative parts with no difficulty and in a very short time. Then he sat back and looked down at the exposed interior of the carbine. While admitting that the toggle-link system worked well and had much to recommend it, John also acknowledged its limitations, chief of which was an inability to handle long, powerful and large caliber bullets. Every time he worked on a Henry or Winchester, the former a forerunner of the Model 1866, he gave thought to the problem, but came up with no answer. Yet he felt sure there must be a way that the lever action system could be made suitable for even the most powerful bullets available.

Not until 1882 would John, or anybody else, come up with a satisfactory answer to the problem the Winchester Repeating Arms Company sought to solve in the matter of their rifles' chief defect. And of all the methods tried, only John's gave Winchester rifles a mechanism capable of handling the largest rounds.

"Are you ready to eat yet?" asked the girl, coming to his table.

"Huh?" John grunted, jolted from his reverie. "Oh sure, thanks. Let me put the side plate on first though."

In the bedroom Cole wiped sweat from his face and let out a long breath. With a sigh of relief Calamity let a hunk of lead clatter on to the top of the small dressing table. Blood ran from the open wound and she studied it for a moment then nodded in satisfaction.

"Go fetch my bag, Solly," she requested. "I'll pack the hole with powdered witch-hazel leaves and stop it bleeding. We'll have to do something about his fever though."

"I've some spicebush and hemlock tea made up," Mrs. Janowska put in.

"That'll do fine," Calamity replied. "Whooee! I'm pleased that's over."

"And me," Cole admitted. "You've done good, Calam."

John looked as Cole came to his table and picked up the girl's bedroll. "Is Joe going to be all right, sir?"

"I sure hope so. Calam dug the bullet out and now she wants to finish it off properly."

With that Cole turned and carried the bedroll into the sickroom. John watched the marshal go, then turned his attention to the food brought by the girl. Travelling all day with nothing more than sandwiches and the pemmican had left John with a sizeable appetite and he tucked into the heaped-up plate of food eagerly. Before he could finish, the sickroom's door opened and Cole followed Calamity out. Together they walked across the main room, Calamity finished buckling on her gunbelt and the marshal carrying her coiled whip. As they drew near, John started to rise to his feet.

"Thanks for bringing the gear in, Johnny," the girl smiled.

"Sure, thanks boy," Cole went on and looked at Calamity. "I need some air after that."

"And me," she admitted. "Let's take a walk down and see that they've tended to the team, shall we? And you'd best finish your supper afore it goes cold, Johnny."

Before John could protest that he no longer felt hungry, or show her the good work performed on the carbine, Calamity walked from the room at Cole's side. As they left the building, Cultus and the elder of the agent's assistants came up.

"Say, marshal," the guard said in a low voice. "Neb here's got a problem."

"What kind of a problem?" Cole inquired, knowing that only something important would make Cultus disclose his identity.

"It's this ways, marshal," the assistant explained, looking embarrassed. "Maybe three month back a feller come through here. Smart-dresser, real pleasant spoken—."

"Go on," Cole prompted.

"He got talking to me after I toted his bags inside, bought me a drink. I reckon he could afford it, being one of the owners of a gold mine out Nevada way—."

"The Golden Eagle Mine?"

"You've heard about it then?" Cultus asked and Neb looked worried.

"I've heard," Cole growled.

"Is it any good?" Neb inquired anxiously.

"Not when, as near as we can figure from the description on the stock, it's plumb in the middle of Lake Tahoe," Cole replied. "How much did he sting you for, Neb?"

"Fifty ten dollar shares and threw in a couple more for good measure," Neb groaned. "You sure it's the same mine, marshal?"

"I only wish I could say I wasn't," Cole answered. "He's spread stock for that mine plumb across the Territory. I've passed word out East and West to try and have him arrested."

"All my savings!" Neb moaned. "He took every lousy, stinking red cent I've managed to save—."

"You and plenty more, brother," Cole said quietly. "I only wish there was something I could do to help."

"Twarn't your fault, marshal," Neb replied. "You'd not took office here then."

"If he's caught and the money's recovered, it'll be shared out," Cole stated, giving all the consolation he could.

"Sure, marshal," Neb answered bitterly. "Come on, Cultus, let's look what damage them blasted Injuns did to Joe's coach."

"How is he, Calam?" Cultus asked.

"He'll likely get by," she replied. "We got the bullet out and he's tough as whang-leather."

"Damn it to hell!" Cole growled as the two men walked away, Neb dragging himself along dejectedly. "I've more respect for an owlhoot who comes to town open and robs with a gun than for any stinking swindler."

"And me," Calamity admitted. "Come on, you look like you need that walk."

"Hell's fire, gal, I feel—."

"Then don't. Like Neb said, you warn't even in the Territory when that jasper sold the fake stock."

"Yeah, but—."

"And you've done all you can to nail his hide to the wall," Calamity interrupted firmly. She took his arm and started his feet moving. "Anyways, you never finished telling me why you go around acting like a preacher."

"Looking like one," he corrected. "There's a difference."

"I'd bet money on that," Calamity grinned. "How'd you start?"

"Like I said, Belle Boyd got evidence against the Deacon for forging and I went after him. He run, killed a feller to steal a hoss and lit out. I caught him seven days' ride from the nearest town and brought him back alive. Then I spent maybe a month 'round him until they'd tried him and stretched his neck. Well, the Deacon was a friendly sort of cuss, he killed spooked not for meanness, and I got to like him. Started to pick up his way of talking. That gave Belle an idea. She reckoned I should pretend to be him, us being much of the same build. So I started dressing like this, spouting bits of the bible. By the time we'd rounded up the whole forging ring, it'd come to be a habit. Made my work easier, too, folks tended to talk more with me dressed like this. So I kept right on doing it, even after I was fetched in here as U.S. marshal."

"I've heard plenty about the Rebel Spy. Is she as tough as you rebs claim?"

"She's smart and a real lady, but she's tough enough when there's need."

"I'd like to meet her," Calamity remarked casually.

Not that her casual tone fooled Cole. He had heard would-be hard-cases use a similar way of speaking when they heard the name of a prominent member of the gun-fighting fraternity and itched to see if he lived up to his reputation of fast drawing.

"Happen you do and you start a fuss with her," grinned Cole, "watch her feet. She fights *à la savate*. That's French kick-fighting like they do in Louisiana."

"I'll mind it," Calamity promised.

Although she did eventually meet the Rebel Spy, circumstances prevented Calamity from testing the other girl's ability in the fighting line.* However Calamity did manage to gain first-hand experience of *savate*, when settling a difference of opinion with a Creole girl, during the trip to New Orleans which wound up with her acting as a decoy for and capturing the murderer who had strangled eight women in the city's parks.†

---

*Told in THE BAD BUNCH.

†Told in THE BULL WHIP BREED.

"I sure hate nosey women who ask questions," the girl went on as they approached the empty hay barn. "So I'm not going to ask why you're on the stage."

"Then I won't tell you there's been some hold-ups out Ratchet Creek way."

"Stages?"

"Nope. Ranchers, local businessmen and the like coming or going from town, nothing big yet."

"Then can't the local sheriff handle it?"

"Maybe," admitted Cole. "But I reckon there's more to it than just a few two-bit stick-ups. I reckon somebody's trying out for the—a big one."

"*A* big one, or *the* big one?" asked Calamity.

"A real big, big one, Calam girl. Just how big I can't tell you. So I figured to ride up and be on hand. Only now this Injun business has come up."

"We licked 'em good, why should they bother you?" Calamity said. "I'll bet they're high-tailing it back to their reservation as fast as the hosses'll run."

"Only the feller who sold them the whiskey's not," Cole reminded her. "And it's him I want. Like the good book says, wine's a mocker and strong drink sure makes them red varmints paint for war."

"*That's* in the Bible?"

"Maybe not them exact words," Cole replied cautiously.

"You reckon you can find whoever sold the whiskey to 'em?"

"Maybe."

"Through that jug?" she went on. "Hell, I've seen hundreds just like it all over the West."

"Peddling whiskey to the Injuns was one of the things I was told to stop when the Governor appointed me," Cole told her. "So I did some nosing around and learned who made most of the stuff that comes here. Saw the bosses of the distilling companies and got their help. We marked the bottom of their kegs secret-like and they sent me a list of where each lot went."

"Helpful," Calamity remarked.

"That and scared thcy'd lose their licenses to brew the stuff," Cole answered. "Trouble being I left the list at my office in Promontory. So I've had to send a telegraph message to my deputy and ask him to check who bought the jug. When I learn that, I'll see how to play the hand."

By that time they had reached the barn's door and halted. "Wonder if there's a golden horseshoe nail inside," Calamity said, gently squeezing Cole's arm. "Mark promised to show me one and never got round to it, so I figured your family owes me."

"We could always take a look," Cole replied and they walked through the door into the darkness. "Say, you know what you was saying about the pieces sticking out in different places?"

"Sure."

"Is that the living truth?"

"Don't you know either?" asked Calamity. "Maybe we ought to find out."

"I never could stand living in doubt," Cole agreed.

A quarter of an hour later Calamity sighed contentedly and whispered, "You Counters are sure some family—I'm pleased to say."

Chapter 8

IT'S SO EASY YOU CAN'T LOSE

ONCE AGAIN CALAMITY HAD INADVERTENTLY TRAM-
pled over John's feelings. Bitter pangs of jealousy
twisted at him and added to his sense of loneliness
as he watched the girl walk from the room with
Cole. Leader by age of a family group of six children, he never lacked company in Ogden and so
felt unhappy at being alone. So he wanted compan-
ionship and considered that Calamity had re-
buffed him. Annoyance at, and disillusionment
with, women in general and Calamity in particular
filled him by the time he ended his solitary meal.

Across the room Thorbold nudged Conway,
nodded in John's direction and said, "He's getting
ready."

"Now?" asked Thorbold.

"Let's just leave him for a spell. If that gal don't come back, he'll be the more willing to come in with us."

"You reckon we ought to go through with it, Wally?" Thorbold said worriedly.

"Why not?" Conway spat back. "If the gal and that damned preacher've gone out for what I figure they have, they won't be around for a spell. There's nobody else here we need worry about."

"Maybe he'll tell them about us."

"And let *her* know he's been took for a sucker? He'd sooner die."

"How about Monique?"

"She's gone to red up and I don't reckon she'll bill in if we offer her a cut of the take," Conway answered, paused for a moment eyeing his companion sardonically and went on, "Of course if you don't want in——."

Greed and worry warred on Thorbold's face, the former winning. "All right, I'm in. Only let's make a start now."

Shrugging, Conway led the way across to John's table. "Hey there, Johnny," he greeted. "You on your own?"

"Sure."

"Mind if we sit along with you?"

"Nope."

"It's hell just sitting 'round with nothing to do, ain't it," Thorbold remarked, drawing out a chair. "Now if we had a deck of cards——."

"Maybe there's one behind the bar," Conway suggested. "I'll go ask."

Although John watched the drummer walk across the room, he did not have a chance to see what went on at the bar. Thorbold nodded to Calamity's carbine and asked if John had mended it. Watching his chance, after ordering drinks from the bartender, Conway slipped the deck of cards which had caught Calamity's eye from his pocket. When he picked up the tray loaded with two schooners of beer and a glass of sarsparilla, he held the cards under its edge. Having been distracted, John failed to see this and accepted that the cards came from behind the bar when Conway dropped them on the table.

"You figure it's any fun playing two-handed, Wally?" Thorbold asked.

"Not much. Maybe you'd like to sit in, Johnny?"

"I haven't played cards much," John replied.

"Let's play banker-and-broker then," Conway suggested.

"I've never played it," John admitted, feeling rather ashamed of his inexperience.

"Hell, it's so easy you can't lose," grinned Thorbold. "I thought everybody knew how to play it."

"I can learn, I reckon," John stated.

"Trouble is," Conway told him. "It's no fun without playing for money."

John might be naive in some matters, but he had heard many times about dishonest gamblers. Yet everything seemed perfectly all right. Neither of the drummers looked like the professional gamblers who passed through Ogden; and the deck of cards retained their sealed wrapper in addition to having, as he believed, come from behind the bar.

"Maybe the *boy* don't play cards for money, Wally," Thorbold remarked.

Already smarting under a sense of injustice at Calamity's desertion, John found the word *"boy"* irritating in the extreme. Sure he might lack years, but he could handle a man's work in the gunsmith's shop and had mended the carbine, a task probably beyond the capabilities of the drummers.

"Sure I do!" he snapped. "Let's have a game."

Exchanging glances, Conway and Thorbold settled down in their chairs. While Thorbold handed around the drinks, Conway asked John to open the deck and stack the cards ready to begin.

"Maybe you'd best take the bank first, Wally," Thorbold suggested. "That way we can show you easier, Johnny."

"Sure," John replied, not certain if such was the accepted thing but unwilling to admit his ignorance.

"It's easy enough," Conway explained as John gave the cards an awkward over-hand stack. "All we do is split the deck into three piles and you two bet the bottom card of the stack you fancy is higher than mine. If it is you win, if not you lose. Ace's high, deuce low."

Despite his brilliance in matters pertaining to guns, John's schooling had been fragmentary. On the face of it, to his way of thinking, the game seemed easy enough and its odds evenly balanced between banker and players.

"I understand," he said, watching Thorbold remove a wallet and drop it on to the table. Not wishing to be out-done, John took out his own wallet, containing twenty dollars given by his father to cover his expenses, and placed it by his glass.

Taking the deck, Conway split it into three even piles.

"I'll have a dollar on the middle," Thorbold announced.

A dollar was, to John, a vast sum of money. However he did not want the men to know it. Acting as nonchalantly as if he did the same kind of thing daily, he pulled a bill from his wallet and laid it on top of the left hand pile of cards in imitation of Thorbold's move.

"Seven of clubs," Thorbold said, raising his pile.

"Nine of hearts," Johnny went on, looking at his bottom card.

"Just to show there's no cheating, I'll split mine," Conway remarked and cut the remaining pile to show the middle card. "Eight of spades. You win, Johnny, but I'm up a dollar on you, Lou."

Never had John made a dollar with so little effort and he felt that gambling had its advantages.

Three more times he won, on the last occasion placing down two dollars instead of one. He became aware that Thorbold doubled the amount bet after each loss and wondered why.

"That's the way to do it, Johnny," the drummer told him, winning the next show of cards while John's two dollars went to Conway. "Double up each time you lose and when you win, it all comes back to you."

Thinking about the matter, John saw that Thorbold spoke the truth. As the dealer paid off at even money, the doubled-up bet brought in the amount already lost and showed a dollar profit. With that in mind, John did not hesitate to place four dollars on his next choice.

"Nine of spades," he said.

"Nine of diamonds," Conway countered. "Ties go to the dealer."

"That's the rules, Johnny," Thorbold confirmed.

Collecting when both he and the player held a card of equal denomination gave the banker an advantage of five and fifteen-seventeenths percent, an edge which showed a profit even in an honest game.

The next pass around of the betting saw John lose and he felt worried as he placed sixteen dollars for his next try.

"King of spades," he said with relief.

"Six of hearts," Conway replied, cutting the cards. "You win."

Counting out sixteen dollars, the drummer

dropped them before Johnny and a grin crossed the youngster's face.

"It's a good system," Thorbold said as Conway insisted on fetching another round of drinks. "I'm going to start betting five dollars, that way I'll get an extra five back when I win instead of one."

"But he's your friend," John protested.

"Not when we're playing cards. Anyways, he can afford to lose."

So, on Conway's return, John placed five dollars down on a pile and won. Sitting back, he wondered how long this kind of thing had been going on. There were times when his father's business did not take five dollars during a day, yet he had won that much at one turn of a pile of cards. The next time, however, John lost. With just a touch of trepidation he piled on ten dollars for the next try and, winning, recouped the loss. Then he lost again, doubled up the bet, lost once more and a third time in a row.

Coming from her room, Monique looked about her. A frown creased her face as she saw the cards and money. On walking over to stand a short distance behind John, she heard something which handed her a shock.

"I'll put forty dollars on the right," John announced.

"Can you cover it if you lose?" Conway demanded.

"Sure I can," John assured him, not especially

worried by the prospect of losing as his previous losses had been swept away by following Thorbold's system.

Worry flickered on Monique's features as she watched the way Conway cut the cards, with particular emphasis at how he gripped them when making the final separation of the pile left to him by the players. She looked around and found the room devoid of possible sources of assistance. Working in saloons taught a girl caution and she could well imagine what would happen to her if she mentioned her suspicions to the drummers without adequate support. There was no sign of Calamity or the "deacon," while the agent and all his staff had disappeared into the kitchen. Adopting a disinterested expression, she sauntered across to the front door and went through it. Maybe Conway and Thorbold would have attached significance to her actions but they hardly noticed her as they approached the climax of the game.

On the porch Monique looked around for some sign of help. Seeing no one, she went to the stables and looked inside to find it empty. Next she made for the corrals and again met with disappointment. Just as she thought of returning and telling the agent of her discovery, she saw two shapes leave the darkened barn.

"Yes sir, Solly," Calamity remarked as she and the marshal stepped into the open. "We sure proved that the bits do sit——."

"Calamity!" Monique called and ran forward. "It's John!"

"What's wrong with him?" Calamity barked.

"Those two drummers have got him playing at banker-and-broker. I think they are using 'humps.' Whichever way, he's losing a lot."

"Is he?" Calamity hissed, her hand going to the whip's handle and she headed for the main building at a rush.

While John knew that a win would once more see him five dollars ahead, he still felt concerned as he realized that he must bet six hundred and forty dollars in order to recover the three hundred and twenty just lost. Yet he knew he must go on. Already his losses had cut deeply into the amount needed to purchase the machinery and its owner had demanded the full one thousand dollars before he would part with it. The only hope was that he would win the next cut of the cards, for he could not double up again should he lose.

Conway exchanged a grin with Thorbold as he riffled the cards. This would be the deciding play, or at least the end of the game. Maybe it was better ended, for at any moment Calamity Jane and the "preacher" might return. Carefully squaring the deck, Conway began to cut it. Again he and Thorbold were so engrossed with the prospect of making easy money that they failed to stay alert. Neither heard the front door open or noticed Calamity and Cole enter.

Something hissed through the air and struck the table close to Conway's hand with a pistol-shot crack, carving a groove in the wood. Thorbold let out a startled yell, jerked backward, overturned his chair and sprawled with it to the floor. No less surprised, Conway thrust his chair from under him and came to his feet. John also rose, his eyes following the lash of the bull whip to its owner. Never had the boy seen such an expression of fury as Calamity's face held as she stalked toward his table with Cole close behind her.

"You stinking, no-good, four-flushing bastards!" she spat at the men, then her voice softened a little. "Pick up your money, Johnny."

"Go ahead, *kid*," Conway sneered. "Pick it up, and then let her wipe your nose for you."

"I'll wipe yours for you!" Calamity shouted and her arm rose, sending the whip's lash curling behind her.

"Easy, sister," Cole said, catching her wrist. "Let me speak with this here miserable sinner for the good of his soul."

"You mind your own damned busi——!" Conway began, dropping his right hand into his jacket pocket.

Before the Colt Pocket Pistol could come out, Cole glided forward and ripped a punch into its owner's belly. Conway let out a strangled croak, folding in the middle for his jaw to meet Cole's rising other hand. Calamity watched approvingly

as the drummer straightened up again to catch
Cole's third blow solidly on the side of the jaw.
From the way the marshal handled himself, it appeared that the Cole branch of the family could do
other things near on as good as the Counters.
Spinning around under the impact of the punch,
Conway crashed into a table which collapsed under his weight, and he measured his length on the
floor.

"Behind you, deacon!" Monique squealed from
the front door.

Whirling around, Calamity and Cole saw Thorbold sitting up and trying to pull the Smith &
Wesson from his pocket.

"He's mine!" Calamity yelled and sprang forward.

Maybe Calamity had never seen a *savate* fighter
in action at that time, but she could still use her
feet. Perhaps not as well as a Creole trained in the
noble art of French foot-boxing, but sufficient for
her own simple needs. Certainly she had no cause
for complaint at the result. Out lashed her right
leg, the toe of her boot driving solidly under Thorbold's jaw. He pitched over, landed flat on his back
and the revolver slid away from his limp fingers;
not that he could have used it right then even had
he kept hold of it.

"What the hell?" Janowska yelled, bursting
from the telegraph room.

At the same moment, also attracted by the

noise, Mrs. Janowska, her daughter, Cultus and the bartender appeared from the kitchen. Cole turned and looked at the agent, then he indicated the cards.

"Your guests were sinning and a mite unrepentant, brother," he said.

Spitting blood, Conway sat up. He saw Cole's attention distracted and began to jerk the Colt from his pocket. Before Calamity, or Cultus for that matter, could either give warning or make a move in the marshal's defense, John took a hand. After completing the repair of Calamity's carbine, he had replaced the bullets in the magazine and fed one into the breech. Springing to the little Winchester, he caught it up, thumbed forward the safety catch and shot from hip high. For all that, the bullet flung up splinters from the floor close to Conway's side and caused him to release the Colt's butt hurriedly so that it slid back into his pocket. Blurring the lever, John sent the empty cartridge case flicking into the air and filled the chamber with a loaded round.

Cole's Rogers & Spencer revolver twisted from the holster as he swung to face Conway. Fear crossed the drummer's face as he stared into the .44 muzzle of the gun and realized that its hammer was held back under Cole's thumb while the marshal's forefinger depressed the trigger.

"W—We were only having a friendly game!" Conway croaked.

"I just bet you were!" Calamity snapped, coiling the whip.

"How much did you lose, boy?" asked Cole, holstering his gun and stepping to the table.

"T-Three hundred and twenty dollars last time, marshal."

"Marshal?" repeated Conway, getting to his feet.

"That's the dismal truth, brother," Cole told him. "If I was called to the church, I sure never heard it and a feller has to live. So I took on as U.S. marshal of Utah Territory."

"There's no law against gambling here," Conway pointed out.

"You're right enough about that," admitted Cole, examining the cards. Then he cut the deck into three piles, gripping the cards at the upper end to do so. "You been doubling up, Johnny?"

"Yes, sir," John replied.

"Then make your pick."

"Y—You mean——?" John gasped, putting down the carbine.

"You started this thing, boy," Cole replied. "Now finish it. Make your pick."

Nobody spoke and John ran the tip of his tongue across his lips. On Calamity and Cole's intervention he hoped that the game might be called null and void, but that did not seem to be the case. Slowly he reached out his hand to touch the left side pile of cards.

"Th—This one," he said and lifted it. "Jack of diamonds."

"Take one for that poor sinner you cruelly abused, which same he was asking for, Calam," Cole continued, nodding in the groaning Thorbold's direction.

Although puzzled at the marshal's attitude, Calamity did not argue. Unless she missed her guess, Cole knew exactly what he was doing and could be relied upon to save John from being swindled out of a large sum of money.

"That poor sinner, who got what he needed, takes the middle," she announced and exposed the bottom card of the central pile. "Ain't he the lucky one, queen of clubs."

"Which leaves you this one," Cole told the scowling Conway. "Only it wouldn't be fair for you to have the bottom card. So I'll just cut it again."

Watched by the others and ignoring Conway's angry glare, Cole split the pile; only he did so by gripping the cards in the center.

"Four of diamonds!" John whooped. "I've won!"

"It sure looks that way," agreed Cole and looked at Conway. "Don't it now, brother?"

"He wins," snarled the drummer.

"Are you headed for Ratchet Creek?"

"No, marshal. I'm leaving the stage at Shadloe and going South."

"Forget it, brother. A man with your talents'd do better back East."

"Are you telling me to get out of the Territory?" Conway asked.

"Right out," agreed Cole. "Like you said, gambling's legal—but the way you play's not gambling, now is it?"

"You mean he was cheating me?" John demanded.

"Let's say you didn't have much chance of winning, boy," Cole replied.

"Why you——!" John began and reached toward the carbine.

"Leave it, son!" Cole ordered. "Mind what the Good Book says, whosoever sheds blood is plumb likely to get the other feller's kinfolk hunting him for evens."

"You've won your money back, Johnny," Calamity went on. "Call it straight and forget it."

"Only remember it next time somebody asks you to play cards with them," Cole continued.

"It's over, Johnny," Calamity said gently.

"For me as well?" growled Conway.

"Not for you, brother," Cole told him. "There's the matter of that table you busted. When you've paid Mrs. Janowska for it you can say it's all over and not before."

Chapter 9

I'M NOT A NICE GAL

~~~

"I STILL DON'T KNOW HOW HE DID IT," JOHN RE-marked after Conway and Thorbold disappeared into their rooms under orders to stay put until morning. "It doesn't seem possible that he could cut the cards he wanted."

"He couldn't," admitted Cole. "Not to cut 'em and say he'd get one certain card. But he could get 'em close enough for what he needed. Take a look at the deck and see if you can find out how."

John did as ordered, picking up the cards and studying them. At first he could see nothing out of the ordinary. Then he looked closer and ran his thumb and forefinger gently down the long edges of the deck. In years to come John would gain a reputation for being able to gauge minute measurements as accurately with his finger and thumb as most men could using a micrometer. Already the Browning "feather touch" had developed sufficiently to let him feel certain irregularities in the cards.

"The sides aren't even," he said wonderingly.

"That's right, they're not," agreed Cole. "Look at a few high cards."

Selecting a ten, jack, queen and king, John examined them closely. "They're thinner in the middle than at the ends."

"You've got real good eyes, boy," complimented Cole. "Now look at some of the low cards."

"These're cut down at the ends," Johnny said after examining a deuce, three and four.

Which, while true enough, did not mean that the alterations could be seen easily. In fact Calamity studied the cards for a long time before confessing that she was unable to detect the trimmed-down sections.

"They're there, sister," Cole told her. "This's what they call a deck of 'belly-strippers' down South."

"I've always heard them called 'humps,'" Monique put in, having stood in the background.

"Say, thanks for telling us about those two jaspers," Calamity remarked.

"I didn't want to see him lose all his money," Monique replied. "Well, I'm going to bed."

Waving away John's attempts to thank her, the

girl walked off to her room. Curiosity brought John's attention back to the cards.

"I may be dumb, but I still don't see how they work," he said.

"Look," Cole answered and gripped the cards in the center to cut them. "It's low, under eight." He showed the three of clubs and replaced the cut section on the deck. Taking hold at the upper end, he raised another portion. "This time I've got a card over eight."

When he made the test, John could see how the "humps" worked. By taking hold of the deck in the center, the banker's fingers closed on the extended edges of the low cards. Not until he gripped at the end of the deck would he come into contact with the higher denominations. By skilled manipulation of the betting, the banker could then arrange to build up his victim's confidence and be certain of winning in the end.

"But Conway let me keep doubling my bets," Johnny pointed out.

"Which ought to have made you suspicious for a start," Cole replied. "When you get old enough to go into saloons, Johnny, you'll see that every game the house runs has a limit. They'll only let you make your bets between two sums of money: twenty-five cents to twenty-five dollars, a dollar to seventy-five, or something. That stops you doubling up and up until luck comes your way and wins for you. Any time you get into a game and they'll let you go on and on doubling up, it's crooked."

"So that's how it's done," John said. "He cuts the cards, then after we've made our bets splits his own pile to win or lose whichever suits the betting."

"That's how it's done," Cole agreed.

"Marshal!" called Janowska from the telegraph room. "It's Promontory."

"I'll be right with you!" Cole replied. "Excuse me, folks."

"You must reckon I'm a real fool, Calam," John remarked as they watched the marshal follow the agent into the room.

"Nope, just young," she told him and laid a gentle hand on his shoulder. "But don't let it worry you. Being young's a thing you'll grow out of in time."

"But——."

"Forget it!" Calamity insisted, then a thought struck her. "Hey, you used my carbine!"

"That feller looked mean and I didn't reckon you'd mind."

"That's not what I meant. You know the fool thing busted on me back at the dip."

"I fixed it for you."

Taking up the little Winchester, Calamity worked its lever and watched the breechblock performing its normal function as smoothly as ever.

"Well I'll swan!" she said, picking up the ejected

bullet and slipping it through the loading slot in the side of the frame.

"I hoped you'd be pleased," John told her.

Something in the boy's attitude drew Calamity's eyes to his face. Suddenly she realized that John's trouble with the drummers stemmed from the way she had treated him earlier. Having suffered the pangs of puppy-love herself, she could imagine how Johnny felt at her apparent indifference. In such a frame of mind he would be ripe to be plucked by the unscrupulous pair. And to top it all, he had put aside his personal feelings for long enough to repair the carbine, making a real fine job of it.

"Let's take a walk outside," she suggested.

"Sure, Calam," John replied eagerly. "Maybe I ought to put the money into the safe until morning before we go."

"It'd be best. That's what I've done with mine."

"*You* have?"

"Hell, yes," lied Calamity. "What do you reckon they built it for?"

After John had crossed to the bar and spoken with Mrs. Janowska, going into the office with the woman, Calamity turned to look at Cole as he walked toward her.

"It's come, Calam," he said.

"Who is it?" she asked.

"Feller called Eli Ehart. He runs a trading post maybe twenty miles to the southwest of here."

"What're you going to do?"

"Pay him a call," Cole replied and a throb of controlled hatred filled his voice. "Show him the error of his ways."

"Need any help?"

"You?"

"*Naw!*" Calamity snorted. "Ole Yeller-hair Custer and the whole blasted 7th U.S. Cavalry."

"I'd admire to have you along, singing the hymns for him and beating time with that whip," Cole assured her. "Only they need a driver for the stage at least as far as Shadloe, comes morning."

"Cultus can do it," Calamity protested.

"And then who'll ride shotgun?"

"Reckon they'll need one?"

"Sister, happen they do, it'll be long gone too late to start remembering that they don't have one aboard."

"And you're going after Ehart alone," Calamity wailed. "You're a——."

"Damned fool, Calam. It runs in the family, ask Cousin Mark. If I wasn't a fool, I wouldn't've become a lawman in the first place. Will you drive the stage?"

"If that's how you want it."

"That's the way it has to be," Cole stated. "Now I'm going to grab a meal and hit the hay. I've got a long ride tomorrow."

"Men!" sighed Calmity as Cole left her. "There's

no living with 'em—but I'm damned if we can live without 'em either."

Collecting her gear, she carried it to the room which she would be sharing with Monique and dumped it on the vacant bed. After telling Monique that she would tippy-toe in later, she left, joined John and suggested that they take a walk down to the corral.

Once outside the building, John found himself with a problem. He felt like a hunter who sought out a grizzly bear, faced it and suddenly realized that he did not know how to shoot. Back home he never bothered much about girls, other than avoiding them as much as possible at church socials and the like. There were always much better things to do in his scanty leisure time: hunting, fishing and other male pastimes shared with his brothers. To make the feeling worse, he believed that he was walking with a mature, sophisticated—not that he knew the word—woman of the world; one who had known many famous men and who most likely knew plenty about making love.

"How'd you like travelling, Johnny?" said Calmity, breaking into his train of thought.

"Fine!" he replied, the word popping out like a cork from a bottle.

"It's not much fun doing it alone, though," she went on. "And not near as much fun as being at home."

"Well not the same kind of fun anyways," John admitted.

"Do you have any brothers and sisters?"

"Sure. My pappy's got three wives."

John spoke defensively. Even at his early age he knew that the Mormons' belief in polygamy formed one of the chief causes of Gentile antagonism to his people.

"It's your folks' way," Calamity replied tolerantly. "How do you kids get on with each other?"

"We don't see much of the older ones, but the rest of us get on. We work and play together just like kids in any family."

Once started on the subject, John gave vent to the homesickness which gnawed at him. He told his companion about his father, the big, stern, yet kindly old man who had taught him all he knew.

"He didn't always like my work though," John admitted. "I was ten when I whomped up my first gun. Made it out of the barrel of an old gun, some wire and odd bits I found around the shop. Used a piece of old plank for a butt. Man, that was some gun. How it never blew up in my face, I'll never know. Know how we got it to fire, me not knowing how to make a trigger and hammer mechanism?"

"No," smiled Calamity.

"Brother Matt and me took a can with some bits of burning coke along, lit a twig from it and touched off the powder through a vent hole in the breech. First time we got a chance to use it, we nailed some dusting prairie chickens. That night Ma told pappy how we come by them and he asked to look at the gun. When I showed it to him, he looked kinda proud and sad. All he said was, 'It's lucky you put that shield round the vent or the flash'd come out and hit you in the face.' Trouble was I knew I could've done better. Next morning I took that gun to bits and threw 'em away."

"And never tried again?" asked Calamity.

"Shucks, yes. I made another gun, a good one, for Brother Matt later on. He still uses it."

"You like working with guns, don't you?"

"I sure do. There're so many things can be done to make them better. I'd sure like to try."

"Such as?" Calamity inquired, impressed by his enthusiasm.

"I don't know. Look at the Winchester, there must be a way it can be made to take the big bullets. There's something else I've been thinking about."

"What's that?"

"You know when you fire off a gun, the way the gas'll make leaves or grass blow if the muzzle's near them?"

"I've seen it," Calamity admitted.

"I keep thinking there ought to be some way that gas could be used," John said soberly. "It's a fool notion I've got."

"A lot of folks had fool notions that paid off," Calamity reminded him. She took his hand, feeling him jump a little. "You're a nice boy, John Moses Browning. A real nice boy."

"I think you're swell too, Calam," he replied huskily.

"Why?" asked Calamity.

"Well, you—I—you——."

"Because I wear men's clothes, cuss like a thirty year cavalry sergeant, handle a whip and drive a wagon?" she suggested as John spluttered to a halt.

"Yes'm," he agreed, wondering how she guessed.

"Those're damned poor reasons for liking a *gal*," Calamity said.

"Maybe, but——."

"Now listen to me, Johnny," Calamity interrupted firmly. "First off, I'm not a nice gal to know. Don't argue. I do things other gals don't, but that cuts two ways. A lot of gals do things that I can't."

"Aw, that's not——," John began.

"Oh yes it is," she corrected. "Right now you think I'm something real special. Only at the bottom you *know* that you couldn't take a gal like me back to home with you."

"My folks would like you," John protested.

"Maybe, but not as one of the family. Your maw'd reckon I was a bad female with designs on her lil boy—And afore you puff up, you'll still be her lil boy when you're growed up and raising a family of your own. That's how mothers are with their sons."

Although John tried to protest, he knew at the bottom of his heart that Calamity spoke the truth. Try as he might, he could not picture the girl, dressed and acting in such a manner, fitting into the staid life of Ogden or being accepted by the town's female population.

"You could be right, Calam," he admitted.

"How old are you, Johnny?"

"Sixteen—nearly."

"And I'm rising twenty," Calamity exaggerated.

This was a point which John had been feeling all the time, nagging deep down behind his thoughts of the girl as the future Mrs. John Moses Browning.

"Oh!" was all he said.

"One of these days, Johnny," Calamity went on, "you'll meet a real nice girl your own age, and who your maw'll like. Then you'll start wondering 'What the hell did I ever see in that ornery ole Calamity Jane?'"

"I'll never think that, Calam," John promised. "You'll always be something real special to m——."

The sound of a soft cough came to their ears. Spinning around, Calamity twisted her right hand palm-out to slide the Colt from its holster and her left hand thrust John into the side of the corral where he would be less visible.

"It's only me, sister," said Cole's voice. "Saw

somebody moving down here and figured to look in on 'em."

"It's only Johnny and me, come down for a breath of fresh air," the girl replied, twirling her gun back into its holster. "We're going back now." A faint grin twisted her face. "When you get to my age, you can't stand all these late nights."

"Aw, you're not all *that* old, Calamity," John assured her. "Is she, marshal?"

"Being a truthful man, I'd have to say 'No' to that," Cole answered. "But she'd a real smart gal and don't you ever forget it, Johnny boy."

"I sure won't!" John assured him, then yawned in a too casual manner. "Reckon I'll be getting back and hunting up my bed."

"And me," Cole said.

"That's all right for the passengers," Calamity growled. "But us drivers've work to do. I'll go take a look at my team for the morning."

"Why don't you go along, marshal?" John inquired. "There might be somebody sneaking around."

"There just might at that," grinned Cole. "And it's my duly sworn duty to protect the lives and property of the law-abiding folks of the Territory."

Watching John saunter back toward the main building, with a jaunty swagger and general air of one who finds growing up to be better than he imagined, Calamity let out a gentle sigh.

"He's a real swell kid, Solly."

"And smart too. I heard what you said to him, Calam. You handled him good."

"Thanks. I figured it'd be best if I set him straight afore he pulled another fool game like with the drummers to impress me."

"You've done it, as smooth and easy as it could've been done."

"Just how long've you been on hand?" demanded Calamity.

"Long enough to hear what you told him. I'd've gone back if you'd been planning to show him— the golden horseshoe nail."

"What in hell sort of gal do you think I am?" Calamity yelped indignantly. "Why Johnny's only a kid."

"And you're rising twenty," grinned Cole. "That's a hell of a rise—and it's the first time I've ever heard a woman lie about her age that way."

"Yah! If you're so smart, how is it that you never proved to me that the bits do stick out different on some of us?" Calamity said.

"You mean we *haven't* proved it?"

"Not to me," Calamity replied.

"All right then," Cole told her. "As soon as you've seen to your hosses, we'll go find out."

Chapter 10

HE'S ONE OF THE SEDGEWELL GANG

~~

"Morning, Johnny," greeted Calamity, coming from the room in which she had spent at least some of the night.

"Hi, Calam," he replied.

For a young man suffering from the effects of his first love affair fizzling out, Johnny appeared to do remarkably well in the eating line. Three eggs and a pile of bacon heaped the plate before him, while a crumb-dotted empty dish showed that the events of the previous night had failed to rob him of his appetite.

Grinning a little, Calamity sat at John's table. Janowska's daughter looked out of the kitchen, ducked back inside and came out soon after carrying Calamity's breakfast on a tray.

"She looks a nice lil gal," Calamity commented as the girl walked away after smiling at John.

"Sure," he replied, trying to sound nonchalant, but blushing.

The appearance of Marshal Cole saved John from further embarrassment. Joining Calamity and the boy, he took a seat. After remarking on the weather, Calamity asked if Cole intended to go through with making a call on Ehart's trading post.

"Yep," the marshal agreed. "Then I'll cut across country to Ratchet Creek. May even meet you on the trail."

"Aren't you coming the rest of the way with us, marshal?" asked John, sounding disappointed.

"Nope. Got to go and see a feller."

"That Ehart's a bad one, my pappy allus says," John warned. "He come to see us one time, wanted pappy to repair a load of old muzzle-loading guns. Most of 'em were dead mules, as pappy calls anything that's not worth mending, and he told old Ehart so. Only Ehart said it didn't matter as long as they worked a mite."

"Did your pappy do it?" asked Cole.

"Nope. He reckoned that they might wind up in the wrong hands and that it wouldn't be right to sic unsafe guns on to even Injuns."

"Smart thinking."

"We heard tell plenty about Ehart after that, marshal," John went on. "Folk say he trades guns and drink to the Injuns and works in with owlhoots."

"You don't want to believe all you hear," Cole remarked. "Or believe it, but don't go around talking to other folks about it until you're sure."

"And not even then unless you're sure you can lick the other feller," Calamity put in.

Monique's arrival caused the subject to be dropped. Yawning and complaining that it was still the middle of the night, although the sun just showed above the eastern horizon, she flopped into a chair at Calamity's side. The talk turned to general subjects while they ate a sizeable and well-cooked breakfast. Much as John wanted to learn of the marshal's business with Ehart, the chance did not arise.

After finishing her breakfast, Calamity paid a visit to Pizen Joe. Although asleep, the fever appeared to have left him and his breathing came more naturally. Calamity knew that sleep would help his recovery and so she left the room without waking the old timer. Leaving the main building, she headed for the corral and found Cultus already supervising the harnessing of the team.

"These aren't the hosses we used yesterday," she remarked.

"Nope," the guard replied. "We change teams here and again at Shadloe."

That meant, as Calamity knew, she must become acquainted with the ways of six new horses. However they had the look of a trained team and the task should not be too difficult, especially as she now had the feel of the coach. With the team harnessed to her satisfaction, Calamity swung on to the box. She soon found her judgment of the horses correct, for they responded in a coordinated group, not as individuals, when she drove them to the front of the main building. Already her two passengers and their baggage waited on the porch. Jumping down, Calamity walked to where John stood with the agent.

"I'm sorry I couldn't put your money into the 'treasure chest,' John," Janowska was saying. "But it's a through box and I don't have a key."

"That's all right, sir," John answered. "It'll be safe enough on the trip and I'm putting it into the safe tonight in Shadloe."

"All aboard," Calamity said. "Take my carbine in with you, Johnny."

"Reckon I'll need it?" the boy grinned.

"I sure hope not," she answered. "How about letting us have the box and mail so we can get rolling, Curly?"

"Damned if you're not starting to sound like ole Joe now," Janowska replied.

"All stage drivers get that way," Cultus commented and stepped on to the porch after walking up from the corral. "Who's going to sign the receipt book, you or me, Calam?"

"It'd save us both some questions and paperwork from the Company if you do it, Cultus," Janowska put in hurriedly.

"You could be right at that," drawled the guard.

Leaving the routine details to Cultus, Calamity watched Cole stroll from the building and approach her.

"Changed your mind about coming along, Solly?" she inquired hopefully.

"I wish I'd enough good sense to do it," he replied. "I'm just going to take my pick of the remuda."

"Take care then," Calamity told him. "I'll be looking for you in Ratchet Creek, unless you catch up with me."

"I'll be there," Cole promised.

Starting the coach and handling the new team commanded all Calamity's attention at first. By the time she felt that she might relax without endangering the coach or its passengers, the way station lay too far behind for her to make out the people outside it.

"Damn it to hell," she muttered. "Why's he have to be so all-fired stubborn and bull-headed?"

"Huh?" grunted Cultus, looking at her and she realized that she must have spoken her thoughts aloud.

"I was talking to me!" she snapped.

However the thought continued to pound at her. She wondered what drove Cole to act in such a manner. Of course any decent, honest lawman would want to stamp out the sale of liquor to the Indians; but Cole appeared to be driven into rash-

ness by his desire to do so. As a trained peace officer he ought to know better than go busting
single-handed into a fuss with a bunch of
whiskey-pedlars. Damn it to hell, he ought to be
taking a well-armed posse along to back his play
when he confronted Ehart—

"Calam!" Cultus barked urgently.

Jerking from her reverie, she saw that the trail
made a curve ahead and concentrated on controlling the team instead of worrying about Cole. If he
did not know what he was doing, he had no right
to be wearing a U.S. marshal's badge. So she settled back and gave her full attention to the work
on hand.

The journey went on without incident, covered
at a good speed behind the fresh team. Conditions
proved so conducive to rapid travel that the sun
had not set when they approached the small town
of Shadloe. Clearly the arrival of the twice weekly
stagecoach headed West rated as an event of importance in the town and most of its citizens stood
along the main, in fact only, street to watch. The
inevitable crowd of loafers gathered before the
Wells Fargo building, prominent among them a
soldier and a civilian sporting a cheap version of
professional gambler's attire. Both smoked large
cigars and looked to have been celebrating some
event.

Seeing Calamity seated on the box, instead of
Pizen Joe or one of the other regular drivers,

caused some comment among the people. The weather had been warm and she had discarded her jacket. Snug-fitting, her shirt did little to hide what lay beneath, while its rolled-up sleeves showed her tanned, strong arms.

Always inclined to grandstand a mite in the presence of an audience, Calamity swung the coach adroitly to a halt before the Wells Fargo office. Then she vaulted from the box, landing on the sidewalk before the agent, with her whip hanging negligently over her right shoulder.

"Where's Pizen Joe?" the agent asked, staring as if he did not believe the evidence of his eyes.

"Got his fool self shot by Arapahoes at the dip out beyond Coon Hollow," the girl replied. "I'm driving until one of your boys can do it."

"There's not one here," the agent told her. "Maybe you'll find one at Ratchet Creek; that's where the runs cross each other and they've a bigger staff than down here."

"Whooee, Fred," whooped the soldier. "Just take a look at how she fills them pants, will you?"

"You should look so good, Wendel," the other man replied. "I bet you got nothing like that in the Army."

"If we have, I've never seen it," Wendel admitted. "I'll bet——."

The nature of his wager would never be discovered. Calamity felt neither guilt nor shame at her choice of clothing. Handling a six-horse wagon in a dress would be next to impossible, to say nothing of all the other tasks her work presented when on the trail. However she objected to being made a laughing-stock by a pair of half-drunk small town loafers; one was a cheap tinhorn and the other's pants legs bore the crimson stripe showing him to be an ordnance corporal, a desk-warmer, not a fighting man, and probably on furlough. Experience had taught her that allowing their kind to take liberties in a small way only led them to greater excesses.

So Calamity turned smoothly toward the pair, measuring the distance with her eye ready to teach them the error of their ways. Swinging her whip free, she sent its lash snaking out in the gambler's direction. Few things in the world were so disconcerting than to have the tip of a bull-whip's lash strike a cigar clenched between the teeth. In addition to the crack of the whip, tobacco sprayed up as if a charge of dynamite had been touched off inside it. Letting out a startled yelp, which also served to spit away the shattered remains of the cigar, the gambler staggered backward. He caught his balance and started to reach for his gun.

Knowing something of the man's reputation of vicious temper, the crowd around him scattered hurriedly. Cultus rose on the box, his shotgun swinging up to hip level and aiming in the man's direction as he drew back the twin hammers. Two clicks sounded, ominously loud despite their lack of volume, and reached the gambler's ears. Any place west of the Mississippi River that particular noise carried a certain significance. Only back in the civilized East was the shotgun regarded as a toy for the rich sportsman who wished to shoot rapidly-flying birds. Out West the shotgun ranked with the Colt and Winchester as a mighty efficient kind of weapon, a fighting man's implement un-equalled in its particular field. Swivelling his eyes upward, the gambler found that the muzzles of Cultus' ten-gauge appeared far larger than their .784 caliber. He also refrained from closing his fingers around the butt of the revolver holstered at his side.

"Don't act any more stupid than you have to, feller," the guard warned. "You're tangling with Calamity Jane."

When most of the crowd had scattered to avoid the possible discharge of the shotgun, they had left exposed to view two men, one of whom would much have preferred to remain in the background and concealed behind the assembled people. Dressed in trail-dirty range clothes, the tall, lean man looked little different from hundreds of others who roamed the western plains. He had a bearded face and his right eye-lid drooped slightly. The second man attracted slightly more attention, wearing a brace of low hanging Colts, as opposed to his companion's one, dressed in a buckskin shirt, U.S. cavalry pants and boots and with shoulder long hair trailing from under a wide-brimmed Stetson hat.

Possibly if the pair had remained still, they might have escaped Cultus's notice. However when the crowd moved, the taller spoke to his companion in a soft but urgent manner. Immediately the second man started to turn from the hitching rail where he had been leaning.

Alert for trouble or hostile action, Cultus caught the movement out of the corner of his eye. Darting a quick glance to check on who had attracted his attention, the guard looked straight at the lean man. Recognition came immediately and, as their eyes met, the lean drifter sent his right hand flying toward the butt of his Colt. Maybe he could not rank among the top class, but he showed better than average ability in the matter of drawing a gun. Out licked his Colt, hammer sliding back under his thumb and finger starting to depress the trigger as the barrel cleared leather.

Fast as the man undoubtedly was, but he had to draw his gun and Cultus already gripped a weapon ready to shoot. Nor did the guard hesitate in acting. Every Wells Fargo messenger could claim to be a fighting man from soda-to-hock, skilled in the use of firearms. Nor did the Company place any restrictions on how its employees acted in defense of their lives or property entrusted in their care. Knowing the man intended to kill him, and why, Cultus acted fast.

Swinging the shotgun away from the gambler, Cultus lined it toward a new mark and squeezed the forward trigger. Flame belched from the left side barrel and nine buckshot balls fanned out. At middle ranges—between where a revolver could make a hit sighted by instinctive alignment and the distance at which a sensible man took a rifle if possible—the shotgun reigned as the ideal weapon. Its balls spread just enough to ensure that most of them struck their mark, without the need to take excessive time in aiming, yet would not separate sufficiently for the individual balls of its pattern to pass harmlessly around the enemy's body. The lean man stood within the ideal distance; but not for long.

Even as his Colt came clear and started to line, seven of the nine balls tore into his chest. He shot backward the width of the sidewalk, cannoned off the wall of the nearest building and went down, the gun clattering from his hand.

For all that he wore two guns, the second man did not stop and make a fight. As soon as Cultus cut loose with the ten gauge, the man deserted his companion by turning to run. Calamity did not know what had sparked off the trouble and wasted no time in asking. Springing forward, she swung her right arm and the whip lash leapt after the fleeing man. Leather coiled around his neck, clamping hold like an anaconda catching its prey. Calamity felt the lash grip and heaved back on the handle. Caught in mid-stride, the man's feet continued moving while the upper section of his torso came to an abrupt halt. With a strangled yell of surprise, he landed flat on his back. When he tried to sit up, Calamity tugged at the whip and flattened him once again.

Shoving open the stagecoach's door and ignoring Monique's advice to stay inside, John sprang out holding Calamity's carbine. Already the crowd, even the gambler and soldier, had taken whatever cover they could find, leaving the boy an unrestricted view. Any youngster raised in the frontier country stood a chance of seeing the occasional dead man, which did not make John any the less susceptible to the horror before him. Seven .34 caliber buckshot balls played havoc when tearing into human flesh and the lean man's chest was far from a pleasant sight. Gulping and feeling sick, John moved to Calamity's side.

"Here!" he said, offering her the carbine.

One glance at the boy's peaked, set face told Calamity all she needed to know. Releasing the whip handle, she took the carbine from him and swung toward her captive.

"Stay down!" she ordered, throwing the lever down then up. "Get back inside, Johnny—and thanks."

"*Mais oui!*" Monique gasped from the door. "Come back, Johnny!"

Calamity spared the girl a quick look and found

her pale but composed. Nodding gratefully to the little singer, she then gave her full attention to the second man.

"Keep him covered, Calam!" Cultus requested.

"He's covered good," she replied.

Resting his shotgun on the seat, Cultus sprang down from the box. As he landed, the Colt slid from his holster. Armed to meet any emergency, he converged with Calamity on the scared-looking man. Running along the street, the town marshal formed the third part of a human triangle gathered about him.

"Maybe now somebody'll tell me what the hell's happening," Calamity said.

"I know that feller I shot," Cultus replied.

"Which same I never figured you took him for a prairie chicken," the girl assured him.

"He's one of the Sedgewell gang."

Calamity could not hold down a low whistle of surprise at the news. Maybe the Sedgewell gang of outlaws did not receive the publicity accorded to the Reno brothers, the James boys or Belle Starr, but they rated higher in the opinion of Utah citizens by virtue of being closer to hand. Ranging through Utah and to the West, Van Sedgewell and his men robbed on a large scale and with considerable planning skill. Unlike lesser gangs, they picked their marks, selecting only such as would show a good profit. One thing they never did was perform a casual robbery that might net them nothing more than eating money.

"What in hell's he doing here?" growled the marshal, worriedly darting a glance at the town's small bank.

"Maybe this gent here'd like to give us the answer," Calamity suggested.

"I'll haul him down to the pokey and ask," promised the marshal.

"We'd best get the box and mail inside," Cultus told Calamity. "I want to be on hand when this feller talks."

"And me," Calamity went on, thinking of Cole's comments about the possibility of a big hold-up being planned.

However the prisoner could give no helpful information. A small-time outlaw, he knew his companion to be a member of the Sedgewell gang and hoped to be taken along to meet its leader. Apart from saying that a man had been headed for Ehart's trading post to collect an important message, the prisoner could add nothing further.

"You reckon he's telling the truth?" the marshal asked as they left the man in a cell.

"I'd reckon he's too scared to do anything else," Calamity replied. "How'd you recognize that other jasper, Cultus?"

"He rode as inside man on a coach I guarded and Sedgewell robbed," the guard explained. "Sat inside like a regular passenger, then threw down on the folks when the gang jumped us. He whomped my head with his gun butt for no reason. So I never forgot what he looked like."

"Getting whomped on the head makes me feel the same way," Calamity admitted. "Only that don't tell us why he came here."

"Maybe he, Sedgewell I mean, aims to rob our bank!" yelped the marshal. "I'd best see about taking on some extra deputies."

"Try that soldier and tinhorn I tangled with," the girl sniffed.

"Hell, Wendel's on furlough and his brother's not civic-minded enough to help out," the town marshal replied.

"Could be that he was just passing through, marshal," Cultus pointed out.

"There's that," the peace officer said in a relieved tone. "I'll just keep a watch on any strangers as come in, though."

After they left the marshal's office, Calamity grinned at Cultus. "It's lucky that you talked him down a mite. Way he was acting, he'd like blow somebody's head off when they walked into the bank to put money in."

"Sedgewell'd have to need money bad to jump a bank like that," Cultus answered. "It's a pity we can't let Marshal Cole know about the message that feller was going to pick up."

"Yeah," Calamity agreed.

Seen in the light of day, the marshal did not appear so imposing and dangerous as when faced over the barrel of a revolver. So Conway felt moved to protest at what he regarded as intolerable treatment.

"The company I work for's not going to like this, marshal," he warned.

"Was I a man given to the sin of betting, brother, I'd lay odds that you don't mention it to 'em," Cole replied calmly. "They might start asking how come you got run out of Utah Territory."

"I'm not sure that you can force me out," Conway snorted.

"*I* am," Cole stated firmly. "There're enough smart card cheats around without amateurs coming in. Anyways, my job's to keep the peace and stop fools like you getting killed. That's why I stopped you travelling on the stage."

"How'd you mean?"

"Happen you'd gone on it, brother, you might've been tempted to take another try at young Johnny's poke. Which same I won't be around to stop Calamity busting the sixth Commandment."

"Huh?" grunted the drummer.

"Thou shall not blow a hole in a cheating skunk's head, except when he's going for his gun. And, mister, if you tried going for it against her, that's just what she'd do. So you just take my friendly and well-meant advice, brother."

"What's that?"

"Get the hell back East and clear of temptation," Cole replied, then his voice took on a harder note. "And don't let me see you in my bailiwick again."

Swinging afork the dun, Cole nodded to Conway and rode away from Coon Hollow. Once clear of Wells Fargo's property he put all thoughts of the drummers out of his head. Despite his somewhat high-handed treatment of them, he doubted if either man would lodge a formal protest against him. Even if they did, there was only one man to whom they could complain. The Governor gave Cole a free hand in all matters concerning his work and, hearing his story, would ignore the drummers' objections.

While riding, Cole wondered if maybe Calamity had been right and he had acted a mite hasty and rash. Perhaps he was allowing his hatred to make him incautious in his dealings with Ehart. Yet it was always the same. He could take a lawman's detached interest in most forms of crime, but never when faced with a case of selling hard liquor to the Indians.

As Calamity guessed, more than the normal desire to do his duty and keep the peace sent Cole riding along toward Ehart's trading post. His whole family and the rest of his small hometown's population had died at the hands of hitherto friendly Tejas Indians inflamed to killing rage by the white man's firewater.

From that day Cole had become the implacable enemy of any man who put whiskey into Indian hands. The sights he had seen in the blackened ruins of the town had turned him to look for revenge. Although he belonged to the Texas Rangers, at that time—during the Civil War—it was a semi-military organization less concerned with hunting law-breakers than in defending the homes of the men on both sides who left to join the fighting. The disbanding of the Rangers and its replacement by the corrupt, vicious State Police of the Davis administration did nothing to make Cole like the Yankees, but he still joined the U.S. Secret Service. While its main function was the apprehension of counterfeiters, the organization gathered information concerning many other crimes. Through the contacts he made, Cole brought to swift justice not only the whiskey pedlars who caused his parents' death but many others of their kind.

Any man who rode with the Texas Rangers in the pre-Davis days learned caution and other valuable lessons which never left him. So, despite his thoughts, Cole remained alert for any hint of danger. The agent at Coon Hollow had described to him the shortest route to Ehart's trading post and he travelled with the inborn sense of direction common among range country men. Nor had

working for the U.S. Secret Service dulled a life-
time's training in matters equine, which allowed
him to get the most out of his horse.

The stone jug taken from the dead Arapaho
bumped against Cole's leg as it dangled from his
saddlehorn. Under his left leg rode a fully loaded
Winchester rifle in the saddleboot. He carried his
belongings in a bedroll, with the exception of a
pair of powerful field glasses that rested in the
saddle's offside pouch. If trouble came, he felt
satisfied that he could meet it in one way or another.

All through the day he rode, with only such
pauses as were needed to rest his horse. He hoped
to time his arrival at Ehart's trading post shortly
after the sun went down, but caught his first sight
of the place somewhat earlier than he expected.
There would be at least half an hour more before
the end of daylight, so he decided to use it in a de-
tailed study of his objective.

Halting the dun at the first sight of the trading
post, he slipped from the saddle and sought cover
for himself and the animal. Using the skill gained
in many raids on hostile Indian encampments, he
concealed the horse, took his field-glasses and
stalked closer to the trading post. A quarter of a
mile away from it he came to a stop and found a
place where he might make unseen study of how
the land lay. Settling down under a bush, in a position that prevented the rays of the setting sun re-

flecting on his glasses' lens, he studied the long, one floor log cabin that housed the trading post. No horses stood before the building, but about a dozen and half that number of mules occupied the two big corrals. The horses interested Cole. With the exception of five, they appeared to be the kind of light-draft animals used to haul Wells Fargo coaches. He decided they would form the teams for the two light wagons under the lean-to by the cabin.

Light wagons using fast teams, an ominous combination, used to ensure rapid transportation of illegal goods. A man who sold whiskey and guns to Indians did not need to take along a vast assortment of goods, the profits on even a small consignment being enormous. So the trader travelled light and fast, relying on his speed to keep him safe from prying eyes.

Two men left the front door of the trading post, causing Cole to turn his glasses in their direction. Walking to the corral, they caught a riding horse each and collected a mule, taking the three animals to the front of the building. While the pair saddled their horses, three more men joined them. One fixed a pack saddle on to the mule and the other two brought out a number of stone whiskey jugs. Even a casual observer might have noticed the significant manner in which the men worked, with frequent careful searching of the surrounding area. To a man of Cole's considerable experience the signs stood plain. The men before him were engaged on some activity they had no desire to be witnessed. Seeing the jugs told him why they wished to be unobserved. Cole doubted if he would be located. As a Ranger he had learned concealment, with his life the stake for failure, against the Comanche and Kiowa Indians, past-masters in finding hidden enemies.

Only one of the men before the trading post looked to have Indian blood and even he failed to spot the hidden watcher. Tall, lean, wearing white man's clothing, but with an eagle feather in the band of his Stetson, the half-breed had been one of the pair who first appeared. The rest of the party were white men and Cole studied them for future reference.

The half-breed's companion and two of the others dressed range fashion and might have been taken for cowboys by the uninitiated. Two were tall, one bearded, the other in need of a shave, the third medium sized, slender and young; naturally all wore holstered revolvers.

Which brought Cole to the last man, most probably Eli Ehart, the marshal decided. Taller than the others, dressed in a high hat and black suit such as a prosperous undertaker might wear, he did not appear to be armed. He had a thin, cadaverous face that looked pale compared with the tanned features of the others. Everything about the last man pointed to his being the employer rather than one of the employed. After setting down the jugs he had brought out, he stood back and watched the others work.

"Two less," Cole grunted, watching the half-breed and his companion mount their horses at the completion of loading the mule. "Thing being how many more of 'em are around?"

Possibly no more. A man engaged in Ehart's kind of trading wanted as few people involved in it as could be arranged. In addition to increasing the overheads, more men raised the chances of capture by the authorities. Cole doubted if the departing pair would return that night, but he still faced odds of three to one. However he had surprise on his side.

For all his hatred of whiskey-pedlars, Cole did not intend to charge in and strike blindly like a rattlesnake tipped out of a gunnysack. He intended to write finish to Ehart's illegal and vicious business, but not at the cost of his own life.

Showing all the patience of Ehart's chief customers, Cole waited for night to fall. He watched the trading post as long as the daylight lasted, seeing the three remaining men at intervals, but no others appeared. At last the sun sank down and darkness crept over the land. Still Cole did not move. Two hours went by before he left his hiding place and returned to the waiting dun. He saddled up and rode openly toward the trading post. No worthwhile cover existed beyond the quarter-of-a-mile point from which he watched the departure of the traders, so he did not try to reach the building unseen. To do so and fail would alert Ehart, while riding in openly ought to make him less suspicious.

Although Cole kept a careful watch, he saw no sign of anybody looking from the lamp-lit windows of the building and its door remained closed. Yet he felt certain that his arrival did not go unnoticed. Leaving the dun at the hitching rail, the rifle and jug still on the saddle, he crossed the porch to the front door. After a quick but fruitless look around, he opened the door and stepped inside.

The big room before him appeared no different from any other trading post in the back country. A rack of rifles stood behind the counter, its contents secured by a strong chain running through the triggerguards, padlocked at one end and firmly stapled to the wall at the other. Goods of an almost limitless variety piled the shelves all around the room. Many of the items on display were clearly aimed at the Indian trade: packets of colored glass beads, cheap, gaudy blankets, knives, axes, cooking pots, boxes of large-headed brass tacks so prized for decorating the woodwork of rifles, shoddy white man's clothing and bargain-rate jewellery. All of which could be sold legally to the red man at a fair profit.

Behind the counter stood the man Cole took to be Ehart. His cadaverous face carried no expression, but he held an Army Colt lined straight at the marshal.

"Howdy, brother," Cole greeted in his most solemn manner. "Do you always greet callers from behind a gun?"

"Only after sundown," the man replied, without lowering the Colt. "Ride far?"

"Out from Coon Hollow at sun-up this morning. I was just set to sage-hen for the night when I saw your lights and come in looking for shelter."

As he spoke, Cole darted a keen glance around the room in search of the other two men and failed to locate them. Nothing about the place seemed out of the ordinary. Even Ehart's precaution with the Colt could be understood, or mistaken for the action of a honest man taking no chances. Outside the dun snorted and moved restlessly.

"You a preacher?" asked the man behind the bar. "Talk up, I'm a mite hard of hearing."

"You might say I am," Cole admitted, finding the plea of deafness hard to reconcile with the man's previous behavior.

"Don't often see a man of the church toting a gun."

"This's a hard land, brother. Even a man of peace needs something to make sure he's left to keep it."

"Now that's the living truth," the man agreed heartily and speaking loudly. "The name's Ehart, deacon. Eli Ehart. I run this place."

At that moment Cole received the answer, or part of it, to the problem of the missing men. A soft footstep in the doorway behind him pointed to at least one of them being outside. Still the Army Colt did not waver out of line, although Ehart looked past Cole in the direction of the open front door.

"He'd got this on his saddle, Uncle Eli," said a voice and the young man walked by carrying the whiskey jug. "It looks like one of our'n."

Even from a distance and through the field glasses Cole had not formed a favorable opinion of the speaker. Seen up close he looked less pre-possessing. His thin face had a blotching of pimples and an expression of vicious weakness. Not all the efforts of a good tailor could hide his weedy physique and the fancy-handled Navy Colt holstered at his side did nothing to make him look dangerous. His mode of addressing Ehart explained why the other hired him.

"A deacon toting a gun and whiskey jug," purred Ehart. "Now there's something you don't often see."

"I tell you this's one that we sold to them Arap——," the young man began.

"Shut your yapper!" Ehart thundered. "God

damn it. If you wasn't the wife's nephew I'd've slit your tongue out years back—and still may do it."

"You want for me to get Salty up here?" said the young man sullenly, nodding toward an open door that led to what appeared to be Ehart's office.

"Yeah," Ehart answered, and looked at Cole. "Where'd you come by the jug?"

"I took it off a dead Arapaho," Cole replied. "And I'm a U.S. marshal, not a travelling preacher."

"Leave Salty down there for a spell, Shadrack!" Ehart ordered.

While the hired man had few scruples, he might object to being a party to the murder of so important a man as a United States marshal. So Ehart acted just as Cole hoped he would. By rescinding the order, he reduced the odds against the marshal; although Cole knew he was still far from out of the woods.

"Take his gun, Shadrack," ordered Ehart and his voice raised a shade as his nephew moved to obey. "Do it from behind, damn you, not between me and him!"

Moving around Cole so as to keep clear of the line of fire, Shadrack took hold of the Rogers & Spencer's butt. Used to the normal type of holster, he tried to lift the gun upward and draw it toward him. Immediately he ran into one of the holster's prime advantages and a vital difference from other gun-rigs. Due to the holster's design, the revolver could only be raised out of the top with difficulty. All drawing back on the gun achieved was to press it more tightly against the grip of the retaining spring.

Shadrack expected no difficulty in removing the revolver, but met it. Before his uncle could bellow abuse at the delay, he moved closer with the intention of using both hands to disarm Cole. That was what the marshal hoped would happen. Clearly Ehart did not want his hired man around until Cole could no longer announce his official position, for the trader darted a glance toward the office's open door and the Colt wavered a shade out of line.

Taking what might be his best, if not only, chance, Cole drove his left elbow with considerable force into Shadrack's solar plexus. A strangled squawk broke from the young man at the impact. His hand left the butt of Cole's gun and he shot backward toward the still open front door. At the same moment Cole flung himself to one side, right hand driving toward the revolver's bell-shaped butt. Attracted by Shadrack's squawk of pain, Ehart swung his attention to the two men. Pure instinct caused the trader to squeeze the Colt's trigger while trying to realign it on Cole. The shot came an instant too soon. Cutting through the left sleeve of Cole's jacket without touching his arm, the bullet buried itself into Shadrack's chest, to send him sprawling out of the door.

Cole twisted his gun free as he fell and fired on landing. A hole appeared in the center of Ehart's forehead. Flung backward, he struck the rifle rack and collapsed out of sight behind the counter. Realizing he need waste no more time on the trader, Cole rolled around to face the front door. A pair of boots rose from the edge of the sidewalk, jerking spasmodically. Cole doubted whether Shadrack possessed sufficient intelligence to try such a ruse to lull his suspicions. With the uncle and nephew both out of the game, that left only Ehart's hired man on the premises.

Coming to his feet, Cole darted into the office and found it empty. Yet the trader expected his man to come from there. From the use of terms "to get Salty up here," and leaving him "down there," Cole concluded the man must be in the cellar. Yet he could see no sign of an entrance to the underground room. The office had luxurious fittings, considering the trading post's location, even down to a couple of rugs on the floor. Even as Cole looked, one of the rugs stirred as if something moved underneath it. Swiftly and silently Cole glided until he stood at the rear of the part of the rug which rose upward.

"What's up, boss?" called a voice from underneath. "I thought I heard shooting."

When no answer came, the trapdoor beneath the rug continued to lift. Cautiously, gun in hand, Salty began to emerge. Waiting until the man's head and shoulders came into sight Cole raised a foot and stamped down hard on the trapdoor. It slammed forward, catching Salty between the shoulders and pinning his upper torso to the floor. Stepping over, Cole landed on Salty's gun hand. A howl broke from the hired man's lips as he opened his fingers and released the weapon. Kicking it away, Cole moved into Salty's view.

"Come on out of it!" the marshal ordered. "Do it any way you want, I'd as soon kill you as not."

Slowly Salty obeyed. One glance at Cole's grim face warned the man that he spoke the truth. For all that Salty no sooner rose than he lunged forward. Perhaps Cole's appearance misled him as it had Ehart, but, like his employer, he soon learned the error of his ways.

Very sensibly, Cole regarded criminals as enemies of society and not as poor misguided victims of circumstances who should be mollycoddled and pampered to show them the error of their ways. So he acted fast, hard and decisively. He might have shot the man, many a peace officer would have done so under the circumstances, but he wished to ask questions. So he jerked the gun clear of Salty's reaching hands to lay its barrel with some force across the man's jaw.

In that respect the Rogers & Spencer revolver excelled its Colt rivals. The bar above the chamber formed a solid link with the barrel. So it stood up to being used as a club; whereas doing so with the contemporary Colts risked a fracture of the locking pin holding frame and barrel sections together.

How effective the Rogers & Spencer proved to be showed in the way Salty crashed to the floor and lay still. Holstering his revolver, Cole took hold of the man by the collar and dragged him into the front of the trading post. At first Cole meant merely to couple Salty to the rifle rack chain, but a shotgun lay on a shelf under the counter and asked for a more secure method of holding the man. Taking a set of handcuffs from his pocket, Cole drew Salty's right arm up through the chain and slipped one link to his wrist. Then he raised the man's right leg and completed the fastening of the handcuffs to the left arm underneath it. Without a glance at Ehart's body, Cole left his prisoner and went down into the cellar.

All the proof he needed lay before Cole's eyes in the lamp-lit basement. Stacks of cheap rifles and a few Winchesters stood by one wall along with powder kegs and an open box of bullets. Rows of whiskey jugs covered part of the floor and a couple of barrels, filled with rain water piped down from above, showed that the trader diluted his liquor to increase his profit margin.

With cold, deadly fury Cole unfastened and upended several jugs. The raw stench of neat whiskey made him cough and he went to the powder kegs. Opening a couple, he coated the rest and the floor around them with powder. Taking the lamp from its hook, he left the cellar.

Moaning and struggling weakly, Salty looked at the marshal. Apprehension crept across the man's face as he watched Cole open two cans of kerosene to pour their contents across the floor.

"Who're you?" Salty croaked.

"U.S. Marshal Cole."

Something of Cole's reputation and his hatred of whiskey pedlars had proceeded him to Utah. Fear twisted the pain from Salty's face as he watched the marshal spread blankets into the inflammable fluid.

"What're you aiming to do?"

"See that this place's never used for selling whiskey to Injuns again."

"Y—You're going to set me loose first?"

"Am I?" asked Cole.

"Y—You're a lawman!" Salty wailed. "You have to——"

"Who'll know what I did?" Cole inquired.

Terror tore into Salty. In the unlikely event that anybody should investigate the destruction of the trading post, they would find only charred remains and no sign that he had been burned alive.

"If I tell you where we got the liquor, will you set me free?" Salty moaned.

"I know where you got it," Cole assured him.

"Will you turn me loose if I tell you where two of our boys went?"

"Maybe."

"And if I give you something else. Something about the Sedgewell gang?"

"Now you're starting to interest me," Cole admitted. "Let's hear it all."

"The boys've gone to meet some of Falling Eagle's Arapahoes down Wind Creek way. The bucks allowed to rob a stage to get money for more firewater."

"Let's have the rest of it."

"I don't know much," Salty groaned. "Eli told me to go down into the cellar when he saw the feller coming, so I never saw him. I heard plenty through a crack in the floor through!"

The latter came hurriedly as Cole started to rise with a gesture of impatience. "What'd you hear?"

"The feller said for Eli to tell Sedgewell his sister said come to Ratchet Creek by the end of the week."

"Whose sister?" demanded Cole.

"Sedgewell's. She's sent messages here for him afore. Now will you turn me loose, marshal?"

"I'm damned if you deserve it," Cole growled and took out the handcuff key.

As Cole opened the left cuff, he caught Salty's thrust-out foot in the chest. Although the man could not put his full weight behind the kick, it landed hard enough to throw the marshal off balance. Tearing his right arm from under the chain, Salty flung himself to and grabbed up the shotgun. Cole drew and fired instinctively, to miss. Yet the bullet came so close that Salty felt its wind on his face. Surprise caused him to step back. His legs struck Ehart's body and he sprawled on to his rump.

Sitting up, Cole saw Salty had been uninjured by the bullet. There could be only one course left to the marshal. Even as the hired hand tired to raise the shotgun, Cole took aim and fired. A .44 bullet ripped into Salty's head and he pitched over dead, the shotgun clattering from his hands.

"You damned fool!" Cole growled, coming to his feet.

Ten minutes later flames licked into the air, forming a funeral pyre for the three bodies and making sure that none of the trading post's goods fell into the wrong hands. Cole spent the night close by, waiting for the return of Ehart's two men. At dawn they had not come and he concluded that their loyalty did not extend to taking chances of being caught by whoever had set fire to their employer's property. Regretfully Cole put aside thoughts of trailing the pair. He knew that he must reach Ratchet Creek before the end of the week and prepare a welcome for the Sedgewell gang.

Chapter 12

DON'T NOBODY ELSE GET CLEVER

"Johnny!" called Calamity Jane as the youngster came from his room at the hotel where he spent the night. "Come with me."

"What's up, Calam?" he asked, for the girl carried a screwdriver and hammer.

"I'm going to put our money someplace safe."

"Huh?"

"That feller Cultus shot belonged to the Sedgewell gang. I don't know if they aim to hit the stage, but I'm taking no chances."

"But my money's in the safe down at the office," John pointed out.

"The agent's there and he'll likely let you have it," Calamity replied.

The girl's guess proved correct. On arrival at the office, they found the agent already on the premises. Showing no curiosity, he opened the safe and handed over John's money. Then the boy and Calamity walked around to where the coach stood ready to be harnessed.

After making sure that they were unobserved, Calamity climbed on to the box. With the screwdriver, she forced up the nails holding the seat cover. Then she took a thick pad of money from her jacket pocket and slipped it under Pizen Joe's cushion.

"Now yours," she told the boy.

"That's a smart idea," he enthused handing over the money.

Carefully arranging the money between the cushion on boards of the seat, Calamity nailed the cover into place. Standing back, she examined her handiwork with a critical eye and decided that it would pass unnoticed.

"It'll do," she said. "Go get your breakfast, Johnny. I'll stay on here and lend Cultus a hand with the team."

The thought that Calamity might take his money after he left never entered John's head as he returned to the hotel. All he felt about the incident was pride in the girl's smart selection of a hiding place. So proud that when he joined Monique at a table in the diningroom he told her of Calamity's scheme to thwart possible robbery.

"Why don't you ask her to put your money with ours?" he suggested.

Monique laughed. "I hardly have enough to bother."

"Calam wouldn't mind if you did," John assured her.

"I'm sure she wouldn't," the little singer answered. "Most of my money was spent on this ring and bracelet, but I doubt if Calamity would like to have them under her when the coach starts bumping along."

Studying the jewellery, John felt inclined to agree. He had a vague idea that the brilliant colorless stones were diamonds, which he had heard about but never seen. What the green stones clustered around the central diamond in the ring or spaced evenly through the bracelet might be, he could not guess. He thought of suggesting that Calamity thought out another hiding place, but before he could, the food arrived and Monique started to eat with pointed concentration. Young John might be, but he could take a hint. Thinking on the matter, he decided that Monique regarded herself as old and experienced enough to care for her own property without outside help.

Not until they stood outside the Wells Fargo office watching Calamity fetching the stagecoach to a halt did Monique mention the subject again.

"Can I give you some advice, Johnny?"

"Sure, Miss Monique."

"Don't mention Calamity's hiding place to anyone else. She wouldn't like it if she knew that you had told me."

"Shucks, you're all right," John stated.

Once again John and Monique found themselves the only passengers. Placing Calamity's carbine in the wall rack, he sat facing it and the girl. Up on the box Calamity started the team moving and the Concord rolled along Shadloe's main street at a fair pace. Watching the last houses of the town fall behind, a thought struck Calamity and caused her to turn to the guard.

"Did you have any trouble with those two yahoos who tangled with us when we pulled in last night?" she asked.

"Nope," Cultus replied. "That great seizer back there might not be smart, but he's got just enough sense to stop trouble starting. So he kept them well clear of me."

"How about that jasper with the feller you shot?"

"If he's wanted, nobody's doing it bad enough to put out a dodger on him. So the marshal figures to let him go sometime this morning when we're well clear of town."

"It'd be best," the girl admitted.

"I wonder how Marshal Cole's doing," Cultus remarked.

"He should've got help afore he went after Ehart," Calamity answered. "Damned fool, going on his lonesome that way."

"I figure he knows what he's doing," Cultus replied. "Now *he* is one real smart lawman."

"Hah! You men allus stick together."

"And you women don't. That's why we're the bosses and run things."

"Maybe you'd like to get off and walk for a spell?" Calamity asked.

"A *man* wouldn't pull a mean game like that 'cause he lost an argument," the guard told her.

On rolled the stagecoach and the more open range of the previous days' travel changed to hilly country with scattered woodland. The trail they followed wound along by the easiest route for the horses. Often it curved and turned around slopes which prevented any sight of what lay on the other side. Calamity studied the changed conditions with disfavor.

"This's good country for a hold-up," she remarked.

"If there's one thing I like, it's a happy driver," Cultus replied. "Yeah, Calam girl, it's damned swell country for a hold-up."

"I never asked," the girl said. "But just what is in the chest?"

"Money for the Ratchet Creek bank," Cultus answered. "And I told you when you first started driving."

"I was hoping that I heard wrong," Calamity said, deciding against admitting that her worries at handling the coach had driven all memory of its "treasure chest" out of her head. "How much?"

"Five thousand simoleons. That's below Sedgewell's usual level. He goes for the big ones."

"He could be needing money," Calamity pointed out.

"You're making me feel happier all the time," Cultus growled.

Swinging the coach around a corner, Calamity saw a large Rocky Mountain mule deer in the center of the trail. A young buck, sleek and carrying plenty of meat. The girl felt her mouth water at the thought of venison, but before she could make any suggestions the deer bounded off the trail and into the trees.

"Why in hell didn't you shoot?" she asked.

"For one thing Wells Fargo don't give me shells to shoot deer," Cultus replied. "And for another, I'm not wanting to let folks know we're around. If they want to hold us up, let 'em work for it."

"Just how much chance is there of anybody jumping us?"

"There's always a chance and the farther we get from Shadloe, the better it gets. Until we start coming close to Ratchet Creek, that is. Sedgewell never hit a coach nearer than six miles to a town. That way, by the time the driver can get in and spread the word, he's long gone."

"Now *you're* making me happy," Calamity said.

"Sedgewell only pulls a raid when he's sure he'll get plenty," Cultus reminded her. "This consignment of money was a last-minute business, nobody knew it was to be sent until just afore we left. I'd say there's been no time for word about it to leak out."

A comforting thought for Calamity; although it might not have been had she known that Sedgewell's sister sent messages to the outlaw leader from Ratchet Creek.

"There's more than Sedgewell's bunch around though," she said.

"Sure, but he's like an old grizzly bear. When he's in an area planning something he passes word around for the small fry to keep clear. That way there's no chance of somebody pulling a small job and getting the law riled up and on the prod."

"They listen to him?"

"Young grizzlies listen to the old boss hewhooper. Them as don't get hurt real bad and fast."

"So you reckon we don't have a thing to worry about?" Calamity asked.

"I wouldn't go that far," Cultus replied. "But I'm a mite easier after seeing Sedgewell's man in town. If he was going to Ehart's place for a message, it's not about us. And if there's a big one in the air, Sedgewell'll already have passed the word."

For all that Cultus kept his shotgun across his knees and remained alert. Nothing happened to disturb the even course of the journey and at last he let out a sigh of relief.

"Only another four miles at most to Ratchet Creek, Calam."

"Be night afore we get there," she replied.

At that time they were driving along the bottom of a winding valley with wood-dotted slopes. Ahead lay a blind corner, but Calamity had passed around so many of them without incident that she hardly gave it a thought. Already she had gained such a control of the stagecoach that she could rely on her instincts to make the turn without the need for conscious thought.

It would be good to see Harry and Sarah Tappet again, she mused. Not only did Dobe Killem send along the means to keep his old friend in business, but the rest of the outfit chipped in——

While Calamity thought, the team felt her controlling pressure on the reins and made the turn. A startled curse broke from the girl's lips as she saw the large rock which stood in the center of the trail. Instantly she hauled back on the reins and raised her leg to boot home the brake as hard as she could. The Concord coach had a good braking system and applying it brought the vehicle to an almost immediate halt on level ground.

Taken by surprise, Cultus pitched in his seat and almost lost his hold of the shotgun. Inside the coach, John shot forward to collide with the opposite wall. Winded, but not otherwise hurt, he sat for a moment dazed by the impact.

"Hands high!" bellowed a voice from the right of the trail.

Fully occupied with controlling the team and retaining her seat, Calamity still threw a glance in the direction of the voice. Coming from the bushes level with the rock, a man lined a twin-barrelled shotgun at the driver's box. He wore a hat slightly too large for him, so that it came down to obscure his hair, and a bandana hid most of his features. Clad in nondescript range clothes, he appeared to be around six foot tall and heavily built, a low hanging Colt at his side.

With her fingers interlaced in the reins and body strained back holding the team, Calamity could do nothing. Cultus caught his balance and made as if to raise the shotgun. From among the trees to the left came the flat crack of a rifle. As his hat spun from his head, Cultus gave a cry of pain. He reared to his feet, then fell forward, struck the rump of the near wheel horse and bounced to the trail. On landing, he lay without a movement.

"Don't nobody else get clever!" warned the masked man in a mumbling, indistinct voice as if he spoke through a mouthful of food.

Curses burst from Calamity's lips as she fought to control the horses, especially the left side animal of the rear pair. Spooked by Cultus falling on to it, the near wheeler reared and plunged in a manner likely to set the rest of the team going. Risking a bullet, Calamity ignored the masked man and used every ounce of her skill to restrain the team.

Shaking his head, John glared out of the window and saw enough to tell him all he needed to know. With a low growl, he started to rise and reached toward Calamity's carbine. Giving a screech of fear, Monique threw her arms around him.

"Save me, Johnny!" she wailed, ignoring the fact that she effectively prevented him from obtaining the means to do so. "I'm so frightened!"

By that time Calamity had calmed the team and glared defiance at the man as she lashed the reins to the brake handle. She still held her whip and measured the distance separating her from the robber.

"Toss your gun and whip away!" he ordered.

"Like he——!" Calamity began, tensing herself to strike.

"In three my pard'll start pumping lead into the coach," the man warned. "One——."

While Calamity did not work for Wells Fargo,

she knew the Company ruled in such cases that
the welfare of the passengers came first. Although
a remarkable robust vehicle in many respects, the
Concord's bodywork had to be made of the light-
est possible materials. The plywood panels lacked
the strength to halt a bullet, even if the second
member of the gang could not see the passengers
through the windows and aim accordingly. So
Calamity knew that she must obey the man. If she
alone had been involved, she might have
gambled—probably would have done in her
anger at the shooting of Cultus. However she
liked John and the little singer too much for her to
chance them being hurt.

"All right!" she said, tossing her whip over her
shoulder and coming to her feet. "I'll do it."

Slowly, using her left hand and keeping the
right well clear of the Colt's butt, she unbuckled
the gunbelt. Holding down the temptation to
make a move, she darted a glance toward the left
in the hope of locating the man who had shot Cultus. At first she saw nothing, then a metallic glint
drew her eyes to where two trees grew close together. A rifle barrel showed between the trunks,
aimed at her, but she could see nothing of whoever
held it.

Realizing the penalty for disobedience, for the
rifle's movement warned her that human hands
still held it, Calamity swung her gunbelt and

tossed it on to the grass at the side of the trail. In that way she hoped to minimize any damage the Colt might receive in its landing.

"Now jump down and walk up here," the man ordered.

"How about the guard?" Calamity asked.

"Leave him," the man answered. "You in the coach, come out with hands raised and empty. One wrong move and this gal here gets a gut full of buckshot."

Much as John wanted to object, or fight, he knew that the chance to do so had passed. Earlier he might have risked using Calamity's carbine, but no longer. Throwing a glare of annoyance at Monique, he thrust open the coach's door and jumped down.

"I'm sor——," he began.

"Shut it!" snarled the masked man. "Get up here, both of you."

Walking forward, John and Monique ranged themselves on either side of Calamity. They had been halted in a position which offered the second robber a clear shot at them from the trees. Satisfied that the trio could no longer pose any threat, the masked man approached with his shotgun held negligently before him in both hands.

Holding down her inclination to jump the man and either hand-scalp him or get shot trying, Calamity studied his appearance for future reference. Despite his size and bulk, he took short steps. His hands seemed smaller than one might expect for his heft and were covered by leather gloves. Every item of his clothing could have been bought off the shelves of almost any general store west of the Mississippi River. Nothing about his gunbelt or the Army Colt in its holster caught the eye. The revolver carried plain varnished walnut grips and the normal case-hardened metal finish given to the majority of its kind.

Then Calamity looked at the shotgun, noticing for the first time what a fine piece it was. Less than ten gauge in caliber, it showed a higher standard of workmanship than usual and ought to be easily recognized if seen again.

At the other side of Monique, John also stared at the shotgun. Only he looked with the eyes of a trained gunsmith and saw far more than Calamity.

"Hey!" he said and started to step toward the man. "That's——!"

With a low snarl, the man swung the shotgun. Its butt crashed into the side of John's jaw, spinning him around and tumbling him to the ground.

"You bastard!" Calamity shouted and lunged at the man.

At the same moment Monique let out a startled gasp and collapsed. She fell in front of Calamity, tripping her. Going down, Calamity tried to break her fall. The man swung in her direction, raising the shotgun and driving it down. Pain tore into Calamity as the metal butt-plate struck her head. For a moment bright lights blazed before her eyes, then everything went black.

Chapter 13

IT WAS HIS GUN

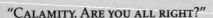

"CALAMITY. ARE YOU ALL RIGHT?"

The words seemed to be coming from a long way off, yet drumming into Calamity's skull as if driven by a hammer. Something cold and wet splashed on to her face and she opened her eyes. Immediately the world started to spin around, while heaving up and down worse than any pitching horse. Slowly it settled and she looked at the scared faces of John and Monique. Weakly Calamity put her hand up and clutched at her throbbing head.

"What——Who hit me?" she groaned, then realization flooded back. "Where's the son of a bitch at?"

"He's gone, they've all gone," Monique replied. "Are you badly hurt?"

Calamity felt at her skull, wincing as she encountered a sizeable lump on it. Twisting her face in pain, she worked her head from side to side.

"I'll do," she answered and tried to rise. "How about Cultus?"

"I—I think he's dead," the singer answered.

"You mean you haven't looked?" Calamity spat out.

"I—I only just recovered from my swoon," Monique replied. "And then I did what I could for you and Johnny——."

Rising, Calamity staggered and John sprang to support her. Despite a swollen jaw, the boy looked in better shape than Calamity. For a moment a wave of dizziness gripped her and as it cleared she started around the coach. Her eyes took in the sight. All the baggage lay on the ground, its contents tipped out in a pile. Near at hand the "treasure chest" stood, padlock shot off and lid open. Calamity did not bother to look inside, knowing she would find it empty. Nor did she think about checking on the hiding place for her own money.

Then she went by the team toward where Cultus sprawled unmoving on the ground. Blood caked the top of his head and Calamity thought him to be dead. Even as the thought came, a groan left the guard and he stirred. Dropping to her knees, Calamity bent over him and a wave of relief hit her. For all that the bullet had grazed his scalp and knocked him unconscious, Cultus could account himself a mighty lucky man. Only an inch lower and the speeding lead would have shattered into his brain.

"Let's have some water, Johnny!" Calamity ordered. "And you'd best get into the coach again, gal."

"W—Why?" Monique gasped.

"I need some more bandages."

"Oh! I see."

Turning, Monique ran to the coach and dived inside. While waiting for the required items, Calamity gave thought to the money hidden beneath the seat. With any luck the owlhoots should have failed to find it. John came up carrying a canteen full of water and a moment later Monique presented Calamity with a white underskirt torn into strips. Swiftly in the fading light Calamity went to work, bathing the blood away and estimating the damage.

"I'm only going to bandage him," she said. "It's near on dark and Ratchet Creek's not far off. We'll put him in the coach and go in."

Anxiety gnawed at John for Cultus' welfare. Unable to stand the strain any longer, the boy walked around the coach and looked up. Then he climbed on to the front wheel and stared at the seat. Its cover had been forced up, Pizen Joe's cushion sticking into sight. Reaching underneath the cushion, John's fingers made a sickening discovery.

"Calam!" he gasped. "They found it!"

Disappointment and rage filled the boy's voice. Turning from her work, Calamity looked at him. Then she glared about her. Soon it would be too dark for any chance of reading tracks. Added to that, it would take time to reach Ratchet Creek. There was no hope of a posse getting on the outlaws' trail before morning.

"I'm sorry, Johnny," she said bitterly, "Only I figured they'd never think to look under there."

A groan from Cultus prevented Calamity from thinking further about the outlaws looking under the seat cover. Giving him her full attention, Calamity completed the bandaging and looked at her companions.

"What do you want us to do, Calamity?" Monique asked.

"We've got to carry him to the coach and get him inside. See they took your jewellery too."

"Oui!" spat the little singer and ripped off a string of what the other guessed to be profanity in French. "And my money from singing. Come, let us start."

Between the three of them, Calamity, Monique and John managed to lift the unconscious guard and get him to the coach. They slid him in and let him lie on the floor between the seats. While John gathered up her belongings and the shotgun,

Calamity dragged Pizen Joe's cushion from off
the box.

"Put this under his head and try to keep him
steady," she ordered. "I'm going to make some
time."

After buckling on her gunbelt, Calamity took
the whip and swung on to the box. Monique and
John collected their property, packing it hurriedly
and crammed Calamity's gear into the warbag.
With everything aboard the coach, Calamity
drove it around the rock. Back on the trail once
more, she started the team moving at a fast pace in
the direction of Ratchet Creek.

It was a lathered, exhausted six horses that
Calamity brought along the town's main street.
Ratchet Creek, sited on a convergence of wagon
and stagecoach routes, at least tripled Shadloe in
size. A lively town, its saloons did good business if
the noise coming from them meant anything. For
all that, a small crowd had gathered at the Wells
Fargo Office. At the forefront of the waiting people stood two men who caught Calamity's eye immediately. The agent, a shortish man with the
appearance of a mild clerk, and the tall, lean, grizzled man wearing range clothes with a sheriff's
badge pinned to his vest, sprang forward as the
coach came to a halt.

"Where's Cultus?" asked the agent.

Despite his appearance, Agent Ray Burkee was
a tough man and capable. So Calamity, having

heard of him from the guard, did not object to the brusque tone.

"Got shot in a hold-up about four mile back," she replied.

"All right, folks, stand back!" ordered the sheriff, raising his voice over the excited chatter that followed Calamity's words.

Watching how the people obeyed, Calamity figured the sheriff to be a far better peace officer than the marshal in Shadloe. Nor did Burkee show any hesitation as he sprang to the coach's nearest door.

"Hey, Monique," he greeted as the singer appeared. "Are you all right?"

"I am unhurt," she replied.

"Go wait in the office," Burkee suggested. "And you, young feller. Some of you come and lend a hand with Cultus."

"You'll be Calamity Jane, huh?" the sheriff said as men obeyed the agent. "Janowska at Coon Hollow telegraphed to say you'd be driving. I'm Ham Jergens. Say, did they hurt you?"

"Whomped me over the head with a rifle," Calamity replied. "Any other place and they might've done some damage."

"You all right?"

"I'll get by, sheriff. I'll see to the team."

"Leave Ray's boys do it. I want to ask you some questions."

Under other conditions Calamity would have strongly objected to leaving the care of her horses to somebody else. She realized that the sheriff acted for the best and raised no protest to accompanying him into the office. There she quickly gave details of the hold-up and described the masked man as best she could.

"Tall, heavy built, walked with shortish steps and toting a fancy scatter," repeated the sheriff. "He's back, huh?"

"You know him?" Calamity growled.

"I sure wish I did. He's plumb ruining my reputation, gal, way he keeps robbing folks hereabouts. Say, Monique, you ought to've recognized him."

"How's that?" Calamity inquired.

"He robbed a friend of mine while we were on a buggy ride," Monique explained. "If it was the same man. I'm not sure it was. He seemed taller and heavier."

"Put you in mind of anybody?" the sheriff asked.

"*Non*. Of course I see so many people," the singer answered. "There were four of them, all tall men and masked."

"Four?"

"*Oui*, sheriff."

"I only saw the one," Calamity admitted when Jergens turned to her. "And a second's rifle after he shot Cultus."

"The others came after he knocked you and Johnny down," Monique told her.

"Don't reckon you saw anything much, boy?" Jergens said, turning to John.

"Only what Calam told you, sir."

Something in the boy's tone brought Calamity's eyes to him. She read indecision on his face and wondered at its cause. However John said no more and the sheriff did not press the point.

"Waal," he said. "There's nothing I can do to-night. Comes morning I'll take a posse out and cut for signs. You folks'd best go get some sleep. Are you stopping in town?"

"I'll be at Harry Tappet's place and Johnny's coming with me," Calamity replied. "If you want me on the posse———."

"I'll send for you," Jergens promised.

"I'm sorry about this, Ray," the girl went on to the agent.

"Is wasn't your fault, Calam and thanks for bringing the coach here," he replied. "Now I'd best go tell the banker we've lost his money."

"He should worry," Jergens grunted. "Wells Fargo'll cover the loss."

Outside the office Calamity found big, white haired old Harry Tappet and his plump, jovial-faced wife waiting. After telling them that she had managed to save Killem's bank draft by hiding it in the lining of her right boot, she asked if John could be accommodated for the night. Not only was the request granted, but Sarah Tappet insisted they returned immediately, so that she could examine their injuries.

Calamity slept well that night and woke late the following morning to find that the posse had already left town. For all that she beat John to it and Sarah stated firmly that he would be left to have his rest out.

"I've got to go see the banker," she said when Sarah suggested taking things easy.

"Harry already handed the draft in."

"I want to see him about young Johnny," Calamity replied. "He's taking it hard, losing the money. His paw set a lot of store in getting that machinery and he reckons he's failed him. What sort of feller's the banker?"

Over breakfast Calamity had explained the reason for John's visit and Sarah's comments about the machinery's owner left no doubts as to his attitude in the matter.

"Dixon Hewes?" Sarah replied. "Smart and real good-looking. Mind you, I reckon his wife's the brains behind the whole shooting match."

"Wives mostly are," Calamity commented.

"Am I denying it?" smiled the woman. "The Heweses drive a hard bargain. Hard but fair."

"That's all I want," Calamity assured her.

On arrival at the bank, Calamity found it possessed something only rarely seen. Behind the teller's counter stood a tall, slim young woman dressed in a plain black frock. Calamity figured the girl to be good looking, despite the fact that she wore steel-rimmed glasses, took her mousy brown hair straight back and avoided even the slight touch of facial make-up permitted to a "good" woman. Given a mite of fixing up, in fact, she would be real pretty.

"*You* wish to see Mr. Hewes?" the girl asked, peering through her glasses at Calamity, who was dressed in her usual manner.

"And soon," Calamity agreed. "Do you tell him, or shall I?"

"What name shall I give?"

"Canary. *Miss* Canary, not that it'll mean a whoop-and-a-holler to him. Say I'm here for Dobe Killem's freight outfit."

Letting out an indignant sniff, the young woman stalked from behind the counter and knocked at a door marked "Private." She entered and came out soon after with surprise and a disapproving frown playing on her face.

"Mr. Hewes will see you now," she said.

On entering the private room, Calamity faced the second most handsome man she had ever seen. With a slender build and not more than five foot ten height, Dixon Hewes could not compare with Mark Counter in the matter of physique; but he ran the blond giant from Texas a close second in handsome features. Looking closer, Calamity decided that Hewes lacked the strength of character Mark showed. His eyes looked a touch baggy, as if he took his pleasures seriously and regular, she concluded. Rising, he held out a small-looking hand to her.

"Good morning, Miss Canary," he said in a pleasant tenor voice. "I trust that you feel no ill-effects from your adventure?"

"Naw. I was lucky, he hit me on the head," she answered and took the chair he offered her. "I came to see you about young Johnny Browning. He—Hey, you've not bought any of this stuff, have you?"

Hewes followed the direction of Calamity's pointing finger to where two elegantly lettered stiff sheets of paper showed from under the other documents on his desk. While she could not claim to dabble in financial matters, Calamity had seen mining stock enough times to recognize it.

"You know the Golden Eagle Mine?" Hewes inquired, looking a shade flustered.

"Only that it don't exist. Some yahoo's been selling this stuff all over the Territory. Did you buy some?"

"Me?—No, of course not!" the banker hurriedly replied, then his face took on a conciliatory smile. "One of my depositors brought these in and asked for my opinion of them. I asked him to leave them with me until I could get a report."

"They're no good, and that's for sure," Calamity told him. "Anybody who paid out good money for them's been slickered."

"How do you know about it?"

"Solly Cole, the U.S. marshal, told me."

Something flickered across Hewes' face, a brief emotion that Calamity could not place.

"Cole," he repeated. "Is he here?"

Figuring the marshal would not want his business discussing, even with the local banker, Calamity shook her head. "He left the stage at Coon Hollow."

"What can I do for you?" Hewes asked.

Calamity told him of John Browning's predicament and asked for financial aid. For a time they discussed it, then a knock sounded at the door and the female teller entered.

"Mr. Burkee is here for the Wells Fargo pay roll, Mr. Hewes," she said.

Opening his desk's drawer, Hewes pulled out a sheaf of money. "Give it to him out of this."

To Calamity it seemed that the girl showed just a touch of surprise at the sight of the money. However she accepted it without a word and left the room.

"You'll think about helping young Johnny?" Calamity asked. "It's money well used."

"I'll think it over and give you an answer," Hewes promised and Calamity stood up. "One thing, Miss Canary——."

"Yep?"

"I'd be obliged if you'd keep quiet about seeing this stock until after I contact Marshal Cole. There may be something I can tell him that will help trace the man who sold it. If word leaks out, it could scare him off."

"You're talking to a gal who knows how to keep a secret," Calamity assured him and walked from the office.

"Howdy, Calam," greeted the Wells Fargo agent, standing at the teller's counter and putting money into his pockets. "Say, the supervisor for this region telegraphed to tell me that you're to have your fare refunded for helping us out."

"I've never refused anybody who wanted to give me my money back," she grinned. "How's Cultus?"

"Still a mite dazed, but he'll pull through," Burkee replied as he counted out the price of the round-trip ticket. "Sheriff's lit out with a posse."

"So I heard," admitted Calamity, taking the money and stuffing it into her hip pocket. "Did you have a driver here?"

"Sure, the coach pulled out on time."

As they left the office Calamity heard her name called. Turning, she saw John Browning running along the street toward her. So she let Burkee walk off and waited until the boy reached her. He seemed excited and not a touch worried, although she attributed the latter to his financial loss.

"Ease off afore you raise a sweat," she told him with a grin. "I've just been in to see the banker——."

"It's him I wanted to see you about," John interrupted. "I've been thinking about it all night and I'm sure I'm right."

"What about?"

"It was his gun that masked man had at the hold up!"

Chapter 14

CONSIDER THE GILDED LILIES IN THAT THERE SALOON

~~~

FOR A MOMENT CALAMITY MADE NO REPLY AS SHE digested the information the boy gave her. Then she looked hard at him and said, "Are you sure?"

"Real sure. That's what I was going to say when the feller hit me."

"Then you want to feel thankful he did. Because if you're wrong, you'd've got into trouble—and if you're right, he'd've killed you."

"You reckon the banker—?" John started hotly.

"What'd I tell you about that?" Calamity snapped.

"I'm sorry, Calam. I kept quiet last night, and wouldn't say anything until after I'd talked to you."

"Let's head back to the Tappet place," Calamity suggested and, as they walked off, continued, "Why'd you say it was the banker's gun?"

"Last time we, pappy and me, were here, the banker brought it to us. The barrels'd got leaded and we cleaned 'em out for him. There's a gun I'd never forget, Calam. It's made by Manton, in London, England. Twelve gauge, got Damascus-twist barrels—only the third set I've ever seen—and the furnishings're something. If I could make a gun like that—."

"Maybe this Manton jasper's a mite older than you," Calamity smiled.

Then the smile died as she remembered that the boy at her side had repaired her carbine, had already made a rifle, and probably knew as much about firearms as most full grown men.

"Could be the gun's been stolen," she went on. "Keep quiet about this until Solly gets here and we'll see what he reckons we ought to do."

Then she told John of her interview with the banker and what she hoped to achieve. At first she wondered if he would be offended at her for billing in on his private business. However John thanked her and admitted that the owner of the machinery had acted as he expected. For once in her life Calamity decided to exercise tact; at least until she found out what the banker aimed to do. If a loan could not be arranged, or the owner sold the machinery before it could, Calamity reckoned she would say to hell with tact and tell him a few things he would not like to know.

Comforted by that thought, she returned to her temporary home. Never one to sit around idle, she insisted on helping Harry Tappet with a few jobs at the corral of the freight outfit he owned. The bank draft from Dobe Killem covered a loan which had been due at the bank, but the stolen money had been intended to supply the old timer with running expenses until work came in.

While working, Calamity thought about the information John had given her and could reach no conclusion. Early in the afternoon Monique came to the corral and suggested, insisted almost, that Calamity came to the Bull Elk Saloon that night as her guest. Never averse to a social evening, Calamity accepted and the little singer departed.

Toward sundown Sheriff Jergens returned with his posse and visited the Tappet house to interview Calamity and John. First he told them of his own results.

"Nothing," he said. "We combed the country for miles around here. Looks like they split up. We could find only two sets of hoss tracks and lost them on the high country trail to Coon Hollow."

In times of heavy rain the trail used by Calamity became impassable, so an alternate route was found. Being harder going for the horses, the high country trail failed to supplant the other in good weather.

"What're you thinking of doing now?" she asked.

"There's not much I can do, gal," Jergens admitted. "Sure I could keep combing the hills, but I'll just be raising sweat and wasting time."

"Do you get much stealing around town, sheriff?"

"No more'n any other place this size. Why?"

"I clean forgot to take my carbine out of the coach last night. Got there this morning and it'd gone——."

"Stolen?"

"Not as it come out," Calamity admitted. "Ray Burkee had it in his office."

"That's one thing nobody's had stolen around here," Jergens said, sounding relieved. "A gun."

That was the information Calamity had been after. If the banker had lost a valuable shotgun, Calamity doubted if he would have kept quiet about it. Which meant John had made a mistake, or——There Calamity stopped. The masked man had been altogether bigger than the banker and had talked in a different manner.

So Calamity kept quiet. If she mentioned John's thoughts on the matter and they proved wrong, Hewes might refuse to make a loan. Part of her argument had been the boy's ability as a gunsmith offering a better than fair chance of the money being repaid.

That night Calamity went to the Bull Elk, Ratchet Creek's best saloon. At first the bartender eyed her unfavorably, but Monique appeared and introduced her. After that everything went smoothly. There was one over-stuffed blonde just asking to get hand-scalped, but Calamity regretfully decided to leave the matter until her head lost its lump from the owlhoot's blow. Monique, appearing in a brief costume that made the male audience overlook any slight inadequacies in her vocal range, sang on the barroom's small stage and went down well.

"I'll have another drink," Calamity told one of the bartenders and pulled out the money Burkee had given her at the bank.

"Monique said your drinks were on her," he answered.

"I need the change to buck the tiger a whirl," Calamity explained and offered him a ten dollar bill. Then she drew it back again, staring hard at a rusty-brown stain on it. "Only I've changed my mind."

Giving a grunt that seemed to say his thoughts on women in bars had been confirmed, the man moved off to attend to a paying customer. Calamity stood for a moment undecided what to do in the light of her discovery. To see the sheriff might be the best action to take, but Solly Cole ought to be along in the near future and she preferred to deal with him. Never a girl to take a gloomy view of life, she refused to even think that Cole could be lying in an unmarked grave at Ehart's trading post. So she would hold off until at least noon the following day before giving the sheriff her information.

"You do not enjoy yourself, Calamity?" Monique asked, joining her after a spirited rendering of a slightly bawdy song.

"Sure. Only that hit on the head's left me a mite shakey. I reckon I'll go and hit the hay."

"But no, you must stay and see the rest of the show."

Monique became so insistent that Calamity agreed to remain for a little longer. It seemed that the little singer wished for Calamity's company, for she stayed at the other girl's side until going on to the stage. While Calamity enjoyed the songs, she felt tired and made up her mind to leave at the end of the session. As Monique left the stage, a couple of men stopped her and gave Calamity a chance to go.

Pausing just outside the batwing doors, Calamity looked in each direction along the dark, almost deserted street. Further along a couple of men entered another saloon, while in the other direction a man and woman walked away. Calamity turned her feet in the direction of the Tappet place.

The bank faced the saloon and Calamity glanced toward it. Any thought she harbored died abruptly as she saw a dark shape in the alley separating the bank from its neighboring building. She had taken only a couple of drinks, not enough to dull her perceptions, and saw enough of the shape to make her feel decidedly uneasy.

From behind her at the end of the saloon came the crash of a revolver shot. Lead slapped into the wall of the bank, causing the dark shape to jerk backward. Then flame spurted from the shape and Calamity heard the distinctive pattering of a shotgun's load striking wood. While the girl did not know if she had walked into a private fuss, she knew better than to remain standing asking questions. One very important thing struck her. The charge of the shotgun across the street had hit the wall just ahead of her.

Flinging herself forward, Calamity landed on the sidewalk, rolled under the hitching rail and dropped to the street. As she landed, her right hand twisted around the comforting ivory handle and slid the Colt from leather. Acting as an innocent by-stander in a gun-fight could prove mighty dangerous and she aimed to discourage any more stray shooting in her direction. Boots thudded as their owner ran along the sidewalk in her direction. Across the street, the dark shape turned to dart back up the alley and out of sight.

"Consider the gilded lilies in that there saloon," said a familiar voice as the boots came to a halt above Calamity's position. "They toil not, neither do they drive a stagecoach; and I'll bet there's not one of 'em could've dived off this sidewalk as neat as you done it."

"Solly!" Calamity yelled. "He's run for it."

"Let's go take a look," Cole suggested, vaulting the hitching rail and landing at her side. "He's been watching the place for near on an hour, might be interesting to see why."

Side by side Calamity and the marshal darted across the street and into the alley. A shot crashed at its other end and lead spanged off the wall close to Cole. Firing on the run, he sent a bullet to the left of the shooter's muzzle blast. At the other side of the alley Calamity saw the shape which shot at them stagger and heard a croak of pain. Then her Colt cracked, for the shape neither fell nor dropped its revolver. An instant later Cole's Rogers & Spencer bellowed, only the marshal took more careful sight. Already starting to spin around from Calamity's bullet, the shape pitched into the wall. Once more the revolver spoke, but the flame from its muzzle slanted toward the ground.

Behind Calamity and Cole voices yelled. Coming to a halt, they stood in silence and listening. Apart from the spasmodic thrashing from the shape sprawled on the ground, they could hear nothing ahead of them.

"We got him," Calamity said.

"Only why'd he use a handgun down here instead of the scatter he cut loose at you with?" Cole inquired.

"Maybe it was only a single-barrel——How'd you mean, he cut loose at me?"

"Like I said, he'd been watching the saloon for around an hour that I know to, sister. Four fellers came out and went by him without getting shot at."

"Just hold it right there and no sudden moves," called a voice, before Calamity could request details of how the marshal came to be on hand at such an opportune moment. "This here's the sheriff talking."

"I'm a man of peace, brother," Cole said over his shoulder. "Only not when some poor sinner starts throwing lead at me."

"That you, Solly?" Jergens demanded, walking forward.

"This's me, brother," admitted the marshal. "Done come to bring light to the heathen and show the sinner the error of his ways."

Already people attracted by the shooting gathered at the mouth of the alley. Turning, Jergens ordered them to stand back. Then, as the citizens obeyed, he followed Calamity and Cole. By the time they arrived, the shape on the ground lay still. Gun in his left hand, Cole used the right to ignite a match on his pants' seat and illuminated the scene.

"Know him, Ham?" asked the marshal, looking down at an unshaven face twisted in lines of agony.

"It's Siwash Kagg," the sheriff answered.

"Who is he?"

"A no-account. Does some meat-hunting, or trapping sometimes, but mostly he just hangs around town living on what he can beg."

"Do you know him, Calam?" Cole inquired, striking another match.

"Never seen him afore," the girl replied. "And afore you ask, he's too short and heavy for that hold-up man. Where-at's his scattergun?"

"Scattergun?" said Jergens, sounding puzzled. "Kagg never had but that old Remington and a Henry rifle."

"Whoever cut loose at me used a scatter," Calamity objected.

"Suppose the sheriff sees to this poor sinner, sister," Cole put in. "You and me can go take a look around the back there."

"Go to it," Jergens agreed. "I'll see you down to my office when you've looked around."

Leaving Jergens, Calamity and Cole went to the back end of the alley and halted to look and listen for signs of the second attacker.

"The other one's gone," Cole remarked.

"You're sure there was another?"

"Sure as sin's for sale in a trail-end town, sister. The jasper who shot at you was some taller and slimmer."

"Say, how'd you come to be on hand at the right time?" Calamity asked.

"I called at Shadloe and spent some time there, then rode on here," Cole explained. "Went to the Tappet house and young Johnny told me where to find you." A grin twisted his face. "Figured I'd best come along and save you from a life of sin. Only when I saw that feller hiding in the alley I waited to see why."

"Which same I'm not sorry you did. Two more steps and I'd've been right in that gun's shot pattern. You figure somebody was trying to gun me?"

"Nobody else but you," agreed the marshal. "Who'd want you dead, Calam?"

"Me?" she yelled. "I don't have an enemy in the world."

"That jasper didn't mistake you for a cottontail rabbit," Cole pointed out.

"I still can't figure who'd want me dead," Calamity insisted. "Say, did you see Ehart."

"I saw him," Cole admitted and told her quickly what had happened at the trading post, finishing, "When I saw that jasper I figured it might be Sedgewell, or one of the gang and waited to see if he met anybody. I hear you had a mite of excitement on the way in."

"Some," she agreed. "Let's go see the sheriff. There's something you and he ought to know—if he's all right."

"I'd trust him with my life," Cole assured her. "What's up?"

Calamity told him of John's theory and found that he approved of her keeping the youngster quiet.

"Not that I don't trust ole Ham," the marshal said. "But it's not a thing wants talking about promiscuous."

"I don't know what the hell that last one was," Calamity said as they started to walk toward the sheriff's office. "But I agree with you."

On arrival at the sheriff's office, Calamity took a seat at the desk and told her story to Jergens. No expression came to his face, but he nodded soberly at the finish.

"Boy knows guns, I'll give you that. But he could be wrong."

"That's what I thought," Calamity admitted. "At first."

"And now?" asked Cole.

Taking out her money, Calamity extracted the ten dollar bill which had attracted her attention at the saloon. Accepting the ten-spot, Cole turned it between his fingers. He studied the paper, coloration and gazed long at the rusty-brown stain on one side.

"It's the real McCoy, Calam."

"Sure. And that blood stain on it's from Johnny Browning's nose back in Promontory."

"Where'd you get it?" demanded the sheriff.

"From Ray Burkee," Calamity replied.

"Ray Burkee?" growled the sheriff.

"And he got it off that gal at the bank, from money Hewes gave her out of the drawer in his desk."

Silence fell on the office while the two men digested the news. At last Cole broke their thought trains. "How about it, Ham?"

"It takes some believing," Jergens breathed. "Anyways, that jasper who pulled the hold-ups looked nothing like Hewes."

"I've seen the Rebel Spy make herself look older, heavier, taller even," Cole pointed out. "Used a gray wig, theatrical face fixings, padding under clothes that were too big for her, thick heels on her boots."

"That feller did step a mite short for his size," Calamity went on. "And his hands were smaller than you'd figure from his heft. I'm not just saying that to make you reckon I'm right, Ham."

"I never figured you were, gal," the sheriff assured her. "This's a shaker for sure though."

"How well do you know Hewes, Ham?" Cole asked.

"He's been hereabouts for the past year or so.

Took over the bank when his missus' uncle, him being the banker then, died. Him and his wife get on well enough with folks, but they don't mix much excepting for business."

"The bank's sound, though?"

"Allus seemed to be."

"You've had a slew of hold-ups hereabouts, from what I hear, Ham."

"Some, Solly, some. Nothing big though."

"Tell us about them," the marshal requested.

"There ain't much to tell. First time was a rancher who drew some money out of the bank to pay for a bunch of hosses. He'd been sparking Monique, that lil——."

"We know her," Cole interrupted.

"Sure, she was on the stage with you," agreed the sheriff. "Well sir, this rancher took Monique out to his place to see the new hosses. Got held up two mile out of town."

"How many men?" asked Calamity.

"One, with a scatter," Jergens answered. "Rancher'd've likely made a fight but Monique got scared and flung her arms 'round his neck. Feller can't do much fancy lead-throwing with a gal hanging on to him. So he sat fast and lost his poke."

"That was the first one," Cole said, glancing at Calamity.

"Next was a prospector come in and changed

some gold for cash money. He wanted to buy a
place out of town that the bank held a note on. So
Millie Hackerstow, her that works at the bank,
took him out to see it. Same feller jumped them,
cleaned the miner out."

"Most miners'd've done some objecting to
that," Calamity remarked.

"So'd this un," Jergens replied. "Only the Hackerstow gal swooned at the sight of the scatter, fell
into his arms. Afore he could loose her, the owlhoot whomped him on the head with the scatter
and when he come to the money'd gone." He
paused, took out a box of cigars from his desk and
offered it to Cole.

"Mind if we smoke, Calam?" asked the marshal.

"I was just going to ask you the same," she answered and the sheriff took the hint. With her cigar going, a sight that brought grins to the men's
faces, she went on, "You never found the feller doing the robbing?"

"Nary a sign, gal," Jergens admitted. "And the
next time he hit, we looked extra hard."

"Why then?" Cole inquired.

"That time the feller was alone and got his
brains blowed out with a rifle to one side of him. A
week later Millie Hackerstow took a cattle-buyer
out to the Box K and he was robbed. Couldn't
chance making a fight with the gal along, as there
was this rifle lined on him from some bushes and
the scatter."

"Has there been a gal along for each robbery?"

"All bar the third, Calam," the sheriff replied.

"Monique and that gal teller each time?"

"Nope. One time it was a couple of gals from the Bull Elk. Next time it was Sally-Mae Bloom from the general store——Only she's Millie Hackerstow's cousin."

"And Monique'd know those gals from the saloon," Cole commented.

"It was her who introduced them to the two jaspers who were robbed," Jergens admitted. "But Sally-Mae Bloom's as honest as the days're long. So's Millie for that matter. And I've never had a complaint against Monique or any of the Bull Elk gals."

"That Monique's a mighty strange lil gal though," Calamity remarked. "She didn't throw a swoon when them Arapahoes jumped us, nor when ole Pizen Joe collapsed. But she does when that feller points a gun her way—and just at the right time to trip me up."

"And she knew where you hid that money, Calam," Cole went on. "I asked Johnny when he told me about the hold-up and he allows he told her——."

"The young foo——!" Calamity began.

"He did it to show how smart you were, because he likes and admires you," Cole told her. "And where in hell're you going?"

The latter came as Calamity started to rise,

sending her chair skidding back with an angry thrust of her knees.

"To the Bull Elk," she spat out. "When I've done with her, that damned Monique's going to wish she'd never been born."

Chapter 15

HE WANTS ME TO GO AWAY WITH HIM

~~~~~~~~~

BEFORE CALAMITY COULD TAKE THREE STEPS, COLE leapt after her. Catching her by the shoulder, he swung her around and back on to the chair.

"It's not Christmas, sister, but let's have peace and good will toward all women," he said. "Or at least let's try thinking afore you start hair-yanking."

"How'd you mean?" Calamity answered.

"You go down there and jump her, you'll get stopped afore you can do any good," Cole explained. "All that you'll manage is to warn Hewes we're on to him and proving against him'll be hard enough without that."

"You never spoke a truer word, Solly," Jergens went on. "There's something neither of yo's spoke about yet, too. Why'd they try to kill you tonight, Calam?"

"Because they reckon I recognized him at the hold-up," she guessed.

"I don't reckon so," Cole answered. "Young John saw just as much as you did. Nope, there has to be some other reason for going after you."

"Could that jasper we had to shoot be the second man?" asked Calamity, a fresh aspect coming to her.

"He could be. Nobody's seen more than the second feller's rifle so far. Only the one with the scatter ever showed his-self," the sheriff answered.

"Why'n't I go talk to Monique?" suggested Calamity hopefully.

"Because you'd get no place doing it," Cole replied. "All you'll do is scare him off."

"That's what Hewes said to me about the feller who's been peddling the fake stock for the Golden Eagle Mine," Calamity said and told of the incident at the banker's office.

"He could be telling the truth," Cole pointed out. "Anyways, I'll see what he tells me about it."

"What brought you out this ways, Solly?" asked the sheriff. "Did you figure on the stage being robbed and get side-tracked by them whiskey pedlars?"

"Nope. I didn't even know the money was aboard. Nobody knew anything about it until the last minute——Except the Wells Fargo supervisor at Promontory and whoever asked for it to be shipped out here."

"Which'd be the banker," Calamity guessed. "He wasn't at the office when we pulled in last night."

"Ray found him in bed," Jergens told them. "I didn't think much about it at first. But it did look a touch strange, him not being on hand to make sure his money come in safe."

"I'd've expected him to be there," Cole agreed. "Say, Ham, I'll need some help tomorrow night."

"You've got it," promised Jergens, after hearing of Sedgewell's rendezvous. "Did that feller at the trading post say whether the message'd been passed on?"

"Nope. Only that some jasper'd brought it. I reckon Cultus cut down the feller who should've gone for it."

"Then if Sedgewell didn't get word, he may not be here."

"Likely, but we'll keep a watch out——."

"Tomorrow's Saturday," Jergens interrupted. "There's allus a fair slew of strangers around town then. We'll just have to hope we're lucky. Say, is that why you've come?"

"Nope," Cole replied. "I'm here to help guard a shipment of fifty thousand dollars in gold going East from a mine."

"So that's it!" Calamity gasped and even the unemotional sheriff's face showed that the news surprised him.

"That's it," Cole agreed. "It's coming here by a special stage, then going on to Promontory. Gets in Wednesday and leaves at sun up Thursday. And it's been arranged that the gold'll be put in the bank's vault for the night as being safer than leaving it at the Wells Fargo office."

"Fifty thousand dollars!" Calamity said. "That's a whole heap of money."

"More than that masked jasper ever stole in one go or all together," the sheriff went on.

"But not more than Sedgewell's taken before now," Cole replied. "A shipment like this's his meat."

"We're going to have to play this careful," Jergens stated. "Anything I can do for you, Solly, just say the word."

"That's all fine and dandy," Calamity snapped. "But I'm more concerned with getting back Johnny's and my money."

"So am I," Cole told her. "And, unless some damned fool gal with red hair spoils everything by going off half-cocked I may be able to do it."

"Now I wonder who you can mean," Calamity grinned. "I'll do whatever you say, deacon."

"I'm counting on it," Cole told her. "And this's what I want you to do."

Listening to Cole's plan, Calamity decided that

it might work. Certainly she felt she could do her part of it.

So next morning she presented herself at the bank shortly after it opened and requested an interview with Hewes. Millie Hackerstow's disapproval was more marked, for Calamity carried her jacket and wore a shirt even tighter-fitting than that of the previous day. Unless Calamity missed her guess, more than a "good" woman's disapproval lay behind Millie's hostile glare as the teller told her to go in to the private office. Nor did Millie offer to close the door as Calamity walked toward Hewes' desk.

"That'll be all, Miss Hackerstow," Hewes said, but his eyes were fixed as if they were magnetized on the front of Calamity's shirt.

Giving an indignant snort, Millie backed out of the room and closed the door with a bang. Calamity grinned and sat on the edge of the desk instead of taking the offered chair.

"I came to see you about that business of young Johnny Browning," she said, eyeing the banker with what she hoped to be frank admiration.

"I haven't had time to think it over, Miss——."

"Why don't you call me 'Calam'?" she purred, leaning toward him. "And there's no real rush. I only came in to see you again."

While talking, Calamity wondered if she might be rushing things a mite. Then she caught a glimpse of a self-satisfied smirk flicker across

Hewes' face and guessed that she was not the first girl to make such a statement to him. From the banker's attitude, he had become accustomed to young women throwing themselves at him and treated her own actions as a matter of course.

"I'm pleased you did," he said. "Who was the man who saved you last night?"

"Solly Cole."

"The U.S. marshal?" Hewes gulped, then his self-assured pose came back fast. "That was fortunate for you."

"He near on lost a deputy," Calamity said. "Not a regular one, but he's took me on to help guard——."

"Yes?" prompted Hewes as Calamity stopped with the air of one who feels she had said more than she should.

"Shucks, you know about the gold shipment, so there's no harm in me telling you. Solly figures I can watch better'n a man as nobody'll figure on me being a deputy."

"You are in his confidence then?"

"We're real close—Not in any wrong way. He don't go in for that kind of thing," Calamity said, fighting to hold down a grin at the last sentence. "Say, is there any place around that I can get me a swim, private like?"

"I always ride about a mile up the stream outside town," Hewes told her. "There's a good hole up that ways."

"Reckon I can find it without getting lost?" Calamity inquired, leaning closer to him.

"It's easy to find," Hewes answered, eyes bugging out a mite as he stared down beneath Calamity's chin. "But perh——."

Hearing the door's handle turn, Calamity swung off the desk and Hewes adopted an attitude of business-like politeness. As Calamity turned, a woman entered the room. Standing the same height as Calamity, the newcomer looked several years older than Hewes. Which did not prevent her from being a tolerable fine piece of female. Raven black hair framed a good-looking face with lines of strength on it. The black suit she wore cost plenty and it fitted a figure which Calamity had to admit looked mighty eye-catching. Built on the lines most admired at that time, with a big bust, slender waist and firm, wide hips, the woman could have been an actress; yet she wore none of the make-up associated with the stage.

"Evalyn, my dear," Hewes greeted. "This is Miss Canary."

"Howdy, Mrs. Hewes," Calamity said.

"Miss Canary," the woman replied distantly. "Dixon, I want to speak to you."

Studying the banker's wife, Calamity could not think why he married her. Then she decided that if Mrs. Hewes had wanted to marry him, he would not have dared refuse. There stood a woman who could run her man, or Calamity had never seen one.

"I was just going," Calamity said. "Sure hope you can do something for young Johnny."

"I'll think about it," Hewes told her. "Possibly I may have something to tell you this afternoon."

"Let's hope you don't decide to wash me away," Calamity replied and winked.

Watched by the frowning female teller, Calamity left the bank. On her return to the Tappet house, she told Marshal Cole of the interview and announced her intention of going to the swimming hole in the afternoon. Cole pointed out that to do so could put her into danger. If the banker had tried to kill her the previous night, she offered him a mighty good chance to improve on his abortive attempt.

Before any more could be said, the sheriff arrived with an important discovery. Making tactful inquiries, he had discovered that Hewes had been with the town preacher and an official of the local Mormon temple at the time of the shooting. That put the banker in the clear. Strangely Cole and Calamity failed to ask one question which might have shed some light on the matter.

To keep John occupied and out of the way, the sheriff found him a number of gun repairs. So he did not see Calamity leave town that afternoon. Following the stream, she found the pool Hewes recommended and waited. Although she had brought along her carbine, Colt and whip, there seemed no need for the precautions. At last she decided that the banker did not intend to come. The water looked inviting, so Calamity peeled off her shirt and undershirt with the intention of taking a swim. Hearing a slight sound, she bent and scooped up her carbine.

"It's only me, Calam," came Hewes' voice and he stepped into view.

Slowly Calamity replaced the carbine and took up her undershirt. "You handed me a shock there," she remarked.

Walking up, feasting his eyes on her naked torso, Hewes pulled the garment from her hands and said, "I thought you'd come for a swim."

The sun had set when Calamity rejoined Cole at the Tappet house.

"What happened?" he demanded.

"Now I'd say that wasn't a gentlemanly question," Calamity grinned. "Tell you one thing, though. He's real interested in what you're aiming to do about guarding that gold shipment. And in you."

"That last shows he's got good taste," the marshal said.

"You're telling *me* about his taste?" Calamity replied. "After I've fed, I'll go to the Bull Elk and see Monique."

"You mind what I told you," growled Cole. "Keep your cotton-picking hands offen her hair."

"Why sure, deacon," grinned Calamity. "I don't feel half so riled at her now."

Monique greeted Calamity warmly enough and asked questions about the shooting as they sat at a table in the saloon. Following the prearranged scheme, Calamity dismissed the affair as an attempt to kill Marshal Cole into which she had wandered by accident.

"Say, I fixed up a loan at the bank for young Johnny," she went on. "Dixon—Banker Hewes's been real helpful."

"You've seen him?" asked Monique, her smile vanishing.

"Sure. We had a real interesting talk this afternoon."

"This afternoon——So that's why——."

"Why what?"

"Nothing!" Monique snorted and pushed back her chair. "I must go and sing."

"That's put a burr in your fancy lil breeches, gal," Calamity thought as the singer stamped away. "Now I'm getting the hell out of here."

All through her act Monique debated to herself how she should handle the situation. Her idea of getting two of the girls to pick a fight with Calamity came to nothing. Guessing how Monique would react, Cole had insisted that Calamity should avoid trouble and leave the Bull Elk before the singer could make any arrangements.

Next day they went on as planned. It being Sunday, Mrs. Tappet invited the Heweses over to supper and suggested that Millie Hackerstow came along. Continuing with her part, Calamity made sure the girl teller knew, or imagined she knew, how things stood with the banker. By the time the guests left, Calamity felt certain that Hewes was carrying on affairs with both Monique and Millie and had used them as aids in the holdups. She also figured that both the girls would take exception to him showing favor to her.

Monday saw Hewes taking Calamity to lunch at the eating house, ostensibly to discuss John's loan, with Millie scowling after them and Monique glaring down from the saloon's balcony. Yet neither girl made any move or complaint that Calamity could see. In fact when she went to the saloon that night, she found Monique to be as friendly as she had been before Calamity had mentioned meeting the banker. The little singer's attitude struck Calamity as just a touch pitying, as if Monique possessed some knowledge she did not and felt superior for it.

"Maybe Hewes's told her he's just using you for what he can learn," Cole suggested when Calamity mentioned the incident to him.

"Could be," Calamity agreed. "What're we going to do now?"

"Nothing tonight. Comes morning we've a meeting with him, Ray Burkee and Ham Jergens to fix up how to protect the gold shipment." He paused and looked at Calamity. "You're still set on going through with your end of it, Calam?"

"Dead set!" she replied. "I've never been robbed afore and it rankles me to know that scent-sniffing dude done it."

"I wish there was some way I could help you."

"Let's ask young Johnny if he can fix something up."

Cole looked at the girl for a time, then asked, "You reckon he can do it—and keep quiet about it after?"

"I'm willing to bet on it," Calamity replied.

"You will be betting on it," Cole pointed out. "And your life's the stake."

Without a moment's hesitation Calamity came to her feet. "I'll go get him in right now."

On her return with John, Calamity explained the full plan. Watching the boy, Cole felt impressed at the way in which he took the news. Lines wrinkled John's forehead as he thought on the problem and asked surprisingly intelligent questions considering his youth. At last he felt that he knew all that was necessary and promised to get down to some hard thinking. Cole promised to obtain anything John might need and warned the boy of the need for complete secrecy. Then the marshal left John to the problem and hoped that an answer might be forthcoming.

The meeting went smoothly enough, with adequate plans made to ensure the shipment's safety during the night in Ratchet Creek and on the journey to Promontory. The U.S. cavalry guard which was to bring it to Ratchet Creek had to return to its parent regiment, but Cole, Burkee and ten men would form a protective screen for the stagecoach. After some discussion it was decided that they would use the high country trail as being less likely to be suspected as their route. Calamity watched the banker and thought she detected a hint of disappointment on his face.

All through Monday and Tuesday Calamity continued to give the impression of being infatuated with the banker. Yet she raised no further hostility on the part of Monique or Millie. Both girls seemed to regard her with a tolerant, pitying manner and she felt sure that Cole had guessed correctly at the reason for their change of attitude.

While the others laid the foundations for their plot, John worked on his part of the affair. As promised, he had all he needed; although some of his requests struck Calamity and Cole as odd. Clearly he did not intend to stick to the bare essentials of Calamity's scheme. Yet, as she watched him work, the girl felt he might have gone off the trail a mite. However she allowed him to carry on, for the basic element of his idea struck her as sound. John worked with that quiet, almost awesome, concentrated manner which would in the future enable him to design and produce the pilot model of an entirely new type of rifle for the Winchester company in thirty days, *including twelve days travelling time between the factory and his home in Ogden.*

On Wednesday afternoon Cole and Calamity visited the banker at his office.

"We've got trouble," the marshal said. "I've just got reliable word that the Hopkins gang're after the shipment."

If Sedgewell had a rival, it was Rule Hopkins. So far the two outlaw gangs had stayed clear of each other's territory. However such a large sum might easily cause Hopkins to break the unspoken truce.

"That's bad!" Hewes gasped.

"It's worse than you think," the marshal went on. "Somebody at the Wells Fargo office's slipping them word of our plans."

"What do you mean to do?" Hewes asked. "I'd say hold up the shipment and ask for military aid."

"Nope," Cole answered. "We're going through with it. Only we'll need your help."

"Anything I can do, I'll do it."

"We aim to send the gold out in the feeder-run coach to Shadloe, in secret."

"But the feeder run doesn't have a guard along," Hewes objected. "If the driver should learn——."

"The driver already knows," Calamity interrupted. "It'll be me."

"But it's risky!" Hewes gasped.

"Nobody but us three here'll know," Cole pointed out. "We'll make the change over here at the bank. I've got it all worked out. The gold'll be loaded in secret on to Calam's stage and done in the open, with fake boxes, on the special."

Listening to the marshal's plan, Hewes admitted that it might stand a chance of working. Not until Calamity and Cole left the bank to make their arrangements did the girl remember about the mining stock. When she asked, Cole told her that the banker had made no mention of it.

"Could be he didn't want to come out and admit he'd been taken for a sucker with it," Calamity remarked, and did not guess how close to the truth she came. "I'm going to see Monique now. You reckon Johnny can do his part with that Millie gal?"

"After what he's fitted up for you, I'd say he can do damned nigh anything he puts his mind to," Cole replied.

On arrival at the saloon, Calamity joined Monique and took satisfaction in the thought of the shock she would hand the little singer. What Calamity aimed to tell her ought to wipe the smug condescension from Monique's face. After a few pieces of casual chatter about nothing in particular, Monique gave the required opening. Calamity figured herself a better than fair poker player, with a face which showed only such emotion as she wished. At that moment she wore a dejected,

worried expression that often came in handy
when bluffing in the noble game.

"You look worried," Monique remarked, studying Calamity's face.

"Look, Monique," she replied. "I need advice——."

"I'll give it if I can," the singer promised.

"It's—There's—Well, I've got a feller real interested in me. He wants me to go away with him."

Watching Monique, although her head remained bowed, Calamity saw the singer stiffen
and show apprehension.

"Why don't you go with him?" Monique inquired in a strained hiss.

"He's married, but his wife's real mean to him.
Only he figures I can handle her happen she hears
and tries to cut up rough. Gee, Monique, he's been
real good to me and I love him. What should I do?"

Only a few weeks before, a saloongirl had come
to Calamity with a similar problem. So she knew
the kind of words to use and even managed to
look the confused girl-in-love well enough to fool
Monique.

"Do?" the singer said hardly louder than a
whisper.

"Sure. He's fixing to meet me at Shadloe when I
get there with the stage feeder-run tomorrow.
Then we'll go East together."

Although seething with fury, Monique managed to hold it in check. "I would say don't go,
Calamity," she gritted out. "But it's your choice."

At almost the same moment Millie Hackerstow stared in disbelief and growing fury at John Browning. He came to ask her advice: "as a bank teller she must be real smart." His problem was what he should do about hearing Calamity and the banker planning to run away together the following day.

Chapter 16

IF YOU WEREN'T HOLDING THAT GUN

"HEY MONIQUE," GREETED CALAMITY AS THE SINGER came toward the feeder-run coach halted outside the Wells Fargo office. "I didn't figure you'd be riding with me this morning."

"I have business in Shadloe," Monique replied and darted a surprised glance at Millie Hacker-stow who already sat inside.

"Then pile in, gal," Calamity said cheerfully, "and I'll get you to it."

The feeder-run coach was a cheaper version of the fabulous Concords which made the major journeys, used to serve smaller towns off the main stage routes. Six horses pulled it, but less spirited animals than those hauling the vehicles on the "Big Run." Nor, as a usual thing, did the feeder-run stagecoach carry an armed guard. Wishing to maintain a normal appearance and avoid attracting attention, it had been decided to dispense with the messenger despite what the coach carried.

Watched by almost all the town, well-armed men had guarded the unloading of the "treasure chests" and stored them in the bank's vault the previous evening. What nobody saw was the arrival of a similar number of identical boxes at the bank's rear entrance in the small hours of the morning. Nor, as far as precautions could make sure, did anyone witness the loading of the first arrivals into the rear boot of the feeder run coach. Down at the bank, again a center of attraction, Cole and the armed deputies supervised the loading of the second lot of boxes on to the special stagecoach.

When the loading had been completed, the coach drew away from the bank. Armed riders formed a circle around the vehicle, with Marshal Cole in the lead. As the party went by, Calamity tagged along in the rear. She felt like a poor relation following the quality at a fancy wedding. Once outside town, the first coach turned on to the high country trail and Calamity continued along the low land route. In one way the poorer quality team helped her, for it did not make a high speed. To keep to the plan she must try to stay level with Cole's party a mile away on the higher ground.

After looking around carefully to make sure she

was not observed, Calamity looped the reins on the box floor and held them with her foot. Then she turned and drew up the tarpaulin cover on the roof. From its shape a casual observer might have concluded that freight of some kind lay underneath. The conclusion was wrong. In throwing back the tarpaulin from the side, Calamity exposed John Browning's invention for protecting her life. At first glance it looked like a Winchester rifle, adjusted to point downward and slightly out from the side of the coach in a forward direction. It rode in two Y-fittings, like some dude's fancy fishing pole on rod-rests, the front one roomy underneath for a good reason. Fitted at the muzzle was a metal funnel, its wide end toward the mouth of the barrel and the spout removed. The funnel rode on slides and a rod ran downward to connect, via a toggle link to the lever. At the rear of the lever, a spring connected it to the butt. Nor did the alterations end there. Built into the triggerguard, a catch depressed the trigger. While the hammer lay back in the firing position, it was prevented from flying forward by a peg between the striker and breech-pin's piston. A cord ran from the peg, through a hole in the driving box and was fastened to the brake handle.

Much thought and hard work had gone into the designing of the weapon and all Calamity's tact had been needed to dissuade John from coming along to see how it worked. Only by explaining that his presence might spoil the whole plan did she manage to keep him out of what would likely be a mighty dangerous situation.

Nothing happened for some time. The team plodded on at a pace Calamity might have found irksome under different conditions. Try as she could, she failed to see any sign of the other party. The idea was that, if Hewes took the bait, Cole and his men would hear the shooting and come charging down to Calamity's rescue. As she approached the scene of the hold-up, things started to go wrong. Wafted on the wind came the sound of distant shooting. Not just a single discharge as might come by accident, or through somebody taking target practice, but a regular fusillade.

Staring upward, Calamity brought her attention to the trail only just in time to see that the rock, removed after the previous hold-up, had been dragged back to the center of the trail. However the team were travelling slowly enough for her to halt them by use of the reins alone. Looking just as big and bulky as before, the masked man rose from behind a rock at the right of the trail. Ignoring him for a moment, Calamity looked to the left and saw the rifle's barrel lined in her direction from behind an oak tree some seventy yards up the gentle slope.

"Raise 'em and no trouble!" mumbled the masked man. "Drop the whip."

"You're wasting your time," Calamity told him. "There's nothing on here worth stealing."

"That's what you say," the man answered and walked forward. "Jump down!"

Which was just what Calamity wanted. After Johnny had fitted the rifle in place that morning on their return from the bank, Calamity looked along its barrel to learn where its bullets would fly. Studying the man, she figured the right moment to be almost on hand.

"Can I put the brake on first?" she asked mildly.

"Do it," he ordered, satisfied that she would obey as she did when told to drop the whip.

Raising her right foot, Calmity waited a second and thrust hard at the brake handle. Doing so pulled on the string and jerked the peg away, allowing the depressed main-spring to propel the hammer on to the breech-pin's piston. Just as effectively as when the trigger was pressed, the hammer struck home and the rifle cracked.

Startled by the unexpected shot and a bullet flying close by his head, the masked man took a hurried step to the rear. He walked into danger. As the gasses from the burning powder gushed out in the wake of the bullet, they struck the inner surface of the funnel and thrust it forward. In turn the movement pulled on the rod which drew down the lever and ejected the empty cartridge case. Then the spring at the rear of the lever contracted and closed the mechanism. In doing so it also caused the catch to engage and force back the trigger. Released from the seat, the hammer flew forward and drove the firing pin against the base of the bullet. Once again powder ignited and lead sped from the barrel. The masked man stepped back into its path. A screech of pain broke from his lips, he jerked under the impact hard enough to throw the hat from his head. Any lingering doubts left Calamity. Even with the bandana still around his lower face, she recognized the banker. Again the rifle cracked as the cycle of mechanical movement cleared the chamber and fed in another round. Hewes spun around as another bullet tore into his shoulder. The two pebbles he had used to disguise his voice rolled from under the bandana as he crashed to the ground.

Expecting at any moment to feel a rifle bullet crash into her, Calamity thrust herself erect. The expected shot sounded from the left, but its bullet drove into the tarpaulin cover. Even as Calamity sprang from the coach, leaping well out to avoid the lead from John's invention, she guessed what had happened. Hearing the shots from under the tarpaulin, the second member of the hold-up thought a hidden guard used it. Instead of shooting Calamity, whoever handled the rifle first tried to silence the more dangerous threat.

"Dixon!" screamed two voices inside the coach as Calamity landed. The door flew open and her passengers erupted, with Millie in the lead.

Without waiting to see what the girls meant to do, Calamity drew her Colt and dived under the coach. On top the rifle fired four more shots before its mechanism broke down, the rod connecting funnel to lever buckling and jamming. Millie sprang to Hewes' side and a moment later Monique joined her. At first the realization did not strike the girls. Then they looked at each other, at first with disbelief, then in fury.

"Get away from my Dixon!" Millie screeched.

"*Your* Dixon!" Monique howled back. "You poor fool, he only used you!"

"It's you he was using!" Millie yelled and slapped the little singer's face.

Rocking back on her heels, Monique let out a squeal like a scalded cat. Then she launched herself across the moaning Hewes full on to Millie and they went down in a hair-grabbing, struggling tangle of flailing arms and waving legs.

Ignoring the sounds of female strife behind her, Calamity prepared to deal with the rifle-user. On one occasion she had seen the Rio Hondo gun wizard, Dusty Fog, demonstrate long range shooting with a revolver. Since then she had practiced the method he used to make hits on a man-sized target at one hundred and fifty yards. While unable to duplicate such super-skilled shooting, Calamity figured she could place her lead close enough at half that distance to at least worry whoever held the rifle.

Naturally one did not stand erect to shoot at

long range. Not even adopting the classic duellist and target-shooter's stance gave a sufficiently steady position for the aiming. Lying prone was the only answer. In fact Calamity also preferred to use a rest. She might have supported the gun on one of the rear wheel's spokes but the horses, while not spooked by the shooting, fiddle-footed enough to make the coach shake and ruined any hope of using part of it. Resting both elbows on the ground, she braced her right wrist with the left hand, then took careful aim. Satisfied, she squeezed the trigger and make the luckiest shot of her life.

Through the haze of powder smoke which followed the explosion of the charge, she saw the rifle suddenly slam aside. On the heels of the bullet's arrival came a startled yelp which Calamity heard despite the cat-squalling noise of the fighting girls behind her. From the pitch of the distant voice Calamity decided that it did not come from a male throat.

Then everything fell into place. Suddenly Calamity remembered a question not asked when Sheriff Jergens brought word of Hewes' alibi after the murder attempt. Neither she nor Cole had thought to ask if the banker's wife had been with him on the night in question. The mystery of the unseen second "man" became clear. Hewes could disguise his appearance to such effect that nobody recognized him, but the same did not apply to his wife. So she remained hidden and backed him up with her rifle.

The realization that she faced another woman cheered Calamity. While she had felt some qualms about tangling with a rifle-armed and desperate man, she figured she could take her chances in a shooting match with any woman. So she hurled herself from under the coach and started a swerving dash toward the tree behind which Hewes' accomplice hid.

Behind Calamity, Monique and Millie tore at each other like a pair of enraged bobcats. Despite her lack of education in such matters, Millie gave as good as she got and the fight showed no signs of abating. Bleeding from the two wounds, the banker lay silent and unconscious.

No shots came at Calamity as she ran up the slope. Skidding around the tree, she saw the rifle lying on the ground. Striking the oak's trunk, her bullet had bounced off to burst the Winchester's magazine tube. Although no bullets had been hit, the magazine spring was broken and thrust out of the ruptured tube. Seeing a rapidly departing back, Calamity realized that her assailant had not stopped to make a fight when finding that the rifle no longer worked.

Racing after the fleeing shape, Calamity knew for certain that she followed another woman. While the running figure wore a Stetson hat, jacket, levis pants and boots, the running style was definitely feminine. Then the shape disappeared into a dip and Calamity went after her. Ahead was a clearing with the trunk of a fallen tree in the center. Beyond it two saddle horses and a pack mule were tied to a sapling. Already Evalyn Hewes had freed one of the horses and swung into its saddle.

Not knowing if Hewes were dead, Calamity wanted Evalyn alive to tell where the money taken from her and John was. So the girl thrust away her Colt and bounded across the clearing. Leaping on to the log, Calamity hurled herself through the air. She hit the side of the horse, grabbing hold of Evalyn's arm and jacket collar. Letting out a shriek of rage, Evalyn tried to throw Calamity off but felt herself dragged out of the saddle. Her Stetson flew through the air and the startled horse lunged away to charge off into the trees.

As soon as Calamity's feet hit the ground, she released her hold and jumped clear. Evalyn lit down on her rump and sat glaring up as Calamity drew the Colt to cover her.

"You sure fell for that," Calamity said. "I don't know what all the shooting was, but I'd bet Solly Cole come through."

"You bitch!" Evalyn hissed, "You lousy, stinking bitch."

"I've been called a whole heap worse," Calamity answered cheerfully. "You sure fell for our trick, though. And for a couple of boxes filled with lead."

"L—Lead?"

"Yep. We met the coach outside town yesterday and changed the boxes over."

"Tricked!" Evalyn spat out, rising and shrugging off the jacket which Calamity had half removed while hauling her from the saddle. "And by a lousy, man-chasing lobby-lizzy like you. If you weren't holding that gun——."

"That's soon altered," Calamity replied, twirling her Colt into leather, unbuckling the belt and tossing it aside.

Like a flash Evalyn jumped forward and drove a punch at Calamity's belly. Against nine girls out of ten it would have been a devastatingly effective attack, coming as a complete surprise. Nor did Calamity, the tenth girl, entirely avoid its effect. Ready for treachery, she started to jerk back as soon as Evalyn moved. The fist caught her in the pit of the stomach and doubled her over; but not with its full, crippling power. Up drove Evalyn's knee, aimed at the center of Calamity's face. Once more the rearward movement saved Calamity from the worst of the attack. Evalyn's knee struck her forehead, flinging her back against the fallen trunk. With a screech of triumph, the woman sprang into the air, her feet driving down in Calamity's direction. Desperately the girl twisted away, feeling Evalyn's boots thud down alongside her body. Then Calamity swung her arm, catching behind Evalyn's knees and hooking her feet from under her. Landing on the trunk, Evalyn bounced from it to the ground.

For a moment Calamity paused, needing to regain her breath. When she dived over the log, she found that the respite had allowed Evalyn to recover also. Landing on the woman's raised feet, Calamity felt herself thrown over. All her skill in riding went into breaking her fall and she landed without injury. Swiftly Calamity rose and charged at Evalyn who was also on her feet. In just thirty seconds the girl knew that she had tangled with as tough a woman as had ever come her way.

Meeting Calamity's rush, Evalyn hit her in the face and caught the girl's knuckles on her mouth. If the older woman wanted to use fists, that suited Calamity and she went at it with both hands. For a time it might have been two men fighting, not skilled pugilists, but a pair of sluggers, for neither Calamity nor Evalyn gave any thought to trying to block the blows which rained at her.

Caught in the breast with a savage hook, Evalyn fell back, moaning in pain. Then she turned and flung herself in the direction of Calamity's gunbelt. Seeing the danger, Calamity dived after her, catching her around the waist and bringing her down. Screeching like a banshee, Evalyn kicked and thrashed. As Calamity tried to drag her away from the gunbelt, she lashed her elbow backward. It struck the girl with agonizing force in the bust. Nausea rushed through Calamity, causing her to loosen her grip. With a surging heave, Evalyn dragged free and scrabbled on hands and knees toward her objective. Desperately Calamity lunged forward to catch hold of Evalyn's ankles. With her fingers almost closing on the butt of Calamity's Colt, the woman felt herself dragged backward. She screamed in frustrated fury, bucking her body against the girl's grip.

Giving a heave, Calamity swung Evalyn away from the Colt and sent her rolling on to her back. Then the girl plunged forward, landing on top of the woman. Fingers dug into hair, tearing at it as they rolled over and over. Sweat half blinded Calamity as she sat astride Evalyn's body and rained blows on the woman's head. At first Evalyn tried to throw her off, clawing at her and ripping the shirt open. Then the woman's struggles weakened until she lay sobbing, limp and unresisting. Slowly Calamity began to rise. Up lashed Evalyn's knees, catching the girl's rump and throwing her forward beyond the other's head. Landing on hands and knees, Calamity turned and saw Evalyn roll across the ground to grab the revolver.

Black hair looking like a tangled wool mop, face twisted with exhaustion and rage, marked with bruises and blood, Evalyn jerked the Colt from its holster and tried to rise. Although every movement called for an intense physical effort, Calamity plunged forward. More by luck than good judgment, her hands closed on Evalyn's right wrist. The Colt crashed, but its barrel was pointing away from Calamity. Again sheer instinct drove her into action. Carrying the trapped wrist up, she pivoted and brought off a near perfect flying-mare throw.

A scream broke from Evalyn as she sailed over Calamity's shoulder. Down she crashed, the base of her spine striking the log with shattering force. Once more a scream broke from her, one of agony. Her head struck the floor and she lay with her gorgeous body trailing across the log, mouth open and working soundlessly.

Swinging around, Calamity prepared to follow up her attack. Hooves drummed in the background as she lurched on wobbling legs toward Evalyn. Bending, Calamity picked up her Colt, staggered and supported herself with both hands on the log.

The swirling waves of dizziness left her and she looked to where Cole was galloping up, followed by two of the guards from the other coach.

"What the hell kept you?" she gasped, as the men leapt from their saddles.

"Damned if we didn't ride slap into the Sedgewell gang up there," Cole replied. "Has she hurt you bad?"

Although Calamity felt that Evalyn had done as

good a job of hurting her as possible, she refused to admit it. "Not as bad as I fixed her."

"How about Hewes?"

"He's by the wagon, shot up bad. You'd best go down and stop those two gals fighting afore they snatch each other bald-headed."

"What about you and her?" Cole demanded, nodding to Evalyn.

"I'm fine," Calamity replied. "And she's not going any place for a spell."

Chapter 17

QUIT LOAFING AND COME

~~~

Sitting in the most comfortable chair of the Tappet house, Calamity had to admit there were times when she had felt better. It was just after ten o'clock at night and every bruise, lump, bite or graze fought to assert itself on her aching frame. Yet she refused to retire until hearing what Cole had to tell her.

"Hewes'll live and he's talking up a storm," the marshal said. "His missus' back wasn't bust, but she's mighty sorry for herself. Not sorry enough to talk. We got all we need from him and the two gals. Including why Mrs. Hewes tried to gun you down outside the Bull Elk."

"Why?" asked Calamity, darting a glance at young John Browning, also an interested listener.

"Because you saw that fake mining stock," the marshal replied.

"You mean he's the one who's been selling it?" John inquired.

"Nope, son. He'd bought some."

"Hell, who'd care about him buying a couple of dud lumps of stock?" Calamity demanded.

"Ten thousand dollars worth, sister," corrected the marshal. "The two you saw were only a lil part of it—and all bought with the bank's money. Him and his wife were scared you might start talking about seeing the stock and get folks wondering how much of it he'd been suckered into buying."

"Even if they lied their way out of it, folks wouldn't be happy about leaving their money in a bank run by a jasper who'd got slickered on dud mining stock," Calamity agreed. "Why didn't they try for me again?"

"Don't worry, sister," Cole told her, "Mrs. Hewes aimed to, until he told her how you were acting as a special deputy. They left you alive so he could work on you and learn about that big gold shipment."

"Which he tried," Calamity said. "Was losing all that money why he started the hold-ups?"

"Sure."

"Were the gals in on it from the start?"

"He reckons not. The first time he worked alone. Only when he saw Monique stop the feller drawing, he got the idea. His wife got on to the money being lost about then. Right after, he sent

Millie out with that miner to see the place the feller wanted to buy. The third time, Mrs. Hewes went along, and they had to kill the feller. So he told her his idea, and she had him use his charm on the two gals. I tell you, Calam, he sounded real pleased it was all over."

"So'd you if you'd had to keep a wife and two gals happy," grinned Calamity. "Lord, I bet he near on died when he had to add me to the pot. Were the first hold-ups so they could get their hands in to take the gold shipment?"

"Nope. They never figured on doing it until Sedgewell didn't show like she sent word for him to."

"She?" John ejaculated. "Was she——?"

"Sedgewell's half-sister. That feller we shot in the alley carried messages between 'em," Cole answered. "Seems like Sedgewell found the banker's niece and her husband, killed them and sent his sister along to take their place. They needed a husband and picked on Hewes——."

"So they could rob the bank?" guessed John.

"That was the idea," agreed Cole. "Only after the Heweses took over they found that the old owner'd been a mighty poor businessman. There was hardly anything left for them to steal. Then Sedgewell got the idea of using the bank to stash the money from his robberies until it was safe to be spent. The ten thousand Hewes lost was part of the loot. So you can see why he had to get it back.

His wife went along with him because she reckoned Sedgewell'd never believe they hadn't helped themselves to the money. They figured that the big gold shipment'd make him forgive if not forget."

"Don't start throwing bits of the bible around," groaned Calamity. "So she sent word to Sedgewell to come and see her on Saturday—."

"Only Cultus killed the jasper who should have collected the message and I stopped any chance of it reaching Sedgewell," Cole replied. "When Sedgewell learned about the trading post burning down, he reckoned to ride over and see his sister. Used the high country trail, figuring there'd be less chance of meeting anybody on it, and rode slap into an armed posse. We got him and all his gang; had to kill him a mite afore the rest saw reason, though."

"How about the two gals?" asked Calamity, thinking of Monique and Millie as she had seen them, tattered, bloody and bruised at the end of what must have been a real rough fight. The battered pair were languishing in cells at the town jail, along with the Heweses and the remnants of the Sedgewell gang.

"They'll go for trial with the rest," Cole answered.

"Do they have to?" John put in.

"Sure, boy."

"Can't you ask the judge to go easy on them?" Calamity suggested. "Hell, a gal in love don't know what she's doing half the time. And Hewes was a mighty easy man to love. I might've gone the same way had I met him afore the robbery. In fact I had to keep telling myself all the time that he was a robbing skunk."

"I'll see what I can do," Cole promised. "That gun idea worked real good, Johnny."

"Naw!" the boy replied. "It was too complicated. There has to be an easier way of doing it——."

"If there is, I'll bet you find it," smiled Calamity, having seen him pay for the machinery with money supplied by Wells Fargo until the bank's affairs could be settled.

At that moment Mrs. Tappet entered the room carrying a buff telegraph message form. "For you, Calam," she said.

Taking the paper, Calamity read it and let out a snort. "Listen to this," she said. "Quit loafing and come back here to help deliver supplies to Fort Sherrard, Dobe Killem."

"That's in Sand Runner's country, Calam," Cole warned, mentioning the current top war chief of the Sioux. "You watch he don't get your scalp, sister."

"I'd bet Calam against Sand Runner or any other old Injun," John announced, eyeing the girl with pride.

"You know something, boy," grinned Marshal Cole. "I feel the same way myself."

What happened when Calamity met Sand Runner is told in TROUBLE TRAIL.